I0722624

Monterey Bay Murder

AMANDA WARREN COZY ANIMAL MYSTERY
BOOK TWO

SEREN STAR GOODE

Dedicated to my family for their support and to readers who love cozy stories. You are the best!

ONE

Stinky Humans

Thick fog rolled along the street, socking in the town and blocking the morning sun. Grok liked patrolling in the fog; it hid his bulk until he was ready to pounce.

"Come to me," he called to his prey, knowing the man running along the pavement below could only hear a rumbling meow. He smirked silently as the sound made the bald man jump and spin, searching the street. The man's black jacket flew open, and Grok took note of the weapon in a holster at his waist.

Why is this human following Amanda?

She was an unremarkable female human with springy hair he'd been told not to bat at. She had the unfortunate profession of aesthetic care of the Canis familiaris. The dogs arrived stinking like they rolled in something dead and left smelling like coconut and citrus. But she was his human, and he wasn't going to lose her like he had the last one. Besides, she was a much better cook than her sister.

Balancing his girth on top of the narrow wooden fence would typically be challenging for a cat his size. But Grok was extraordinary. With an almost supernatural agility, he could move undetected by his targets. He had a mastery over fear and was intuitive and stealthy. He was—stuck.

Grok pulled at the boards in the extended privacy fence he was trying to pass through. A vine plant had grown through the hole since he previously used this pass, or last night's third helping of fish and chips had been a mistake.

But you should never regret great food.

Grok popped free like a cork from a bottle and raced to cut off his target.

Usually, the humans on this planet were easy to stalk. They clopped around and ate stinky food. This one was stealthier than most and would have made this morning's adventure an entertaining challenge if not for the pungent aroma of fungi and garlic oozing from his pores.

Grok's paws kneaded the top of the brick wall as he crouched overhead, watching the prey hurry past. Tail twitching, he readied himself.

As if sensing he was about to get a reckoning from above, the man in black darted across the street and jumped into a car.

Before Grok could wiggle his whiskers, the man drove off, his vehicle weaving as he took a corner too fast.

Grok growled. His stomach echoed the call, reminding him they had left the house before breakfast this morning. He had better get back to Amanda and tell her he was right again—someone *had* been watching them.

TWO

No Breakfast

Amanda tried to breathe through her mouth as she studied the clumps of dirt in the hair of the Golden Retriever on her table.

"I don't know what happened." The woman beside her shook her head, her voice nasally as she pinched her nose.

Buddy gave a quick, happy dance, oblivious to his smell. The bits of kelp and sand dropping from his fur sounded like rain as they hit the table.

"I just turned my back for a minute, and he slipped his collar and dove into the water after a seal. It was hard to see because it wasn't dawn yet, but it looked like they were playing." Katrina stamped her foot and narrowed her eyes at the dog, who wagged his tail.

Amanda's eyes watered. She desperately wanted to cover her nose with a mask until she could dig out the nose clip she used with rescue dogs. But would Katrina be insulted? Breathing from her mouth, she gasped, "No problem. We will get him sorted. Is your show in San Francisco?"

"Yes. If we ever make it. At least it's close to Ocean Wood, just two hours up the coast. Buddy doesn't perform. He provides emotional support for his sister Brenda, who doesn't show until tomorrow afternoon, but we have so much to set up and he needs to not stink. Are you okay if I keep packing?" At Amanda's nod, Katrina slipped out the door of the RV.

Amanda could hear her taking deep breaths on the sidewalk.

When the doggy mom left, Amanda grabbed a mask, holding it to her face as she slipped the loops over her ears. The air now filtered to a tolerable level, she took a minute to breathe deep before she got to work.

Her mind wandered as she washed and dried the dog. She didn't know many people in town and owed most of her new clients to Katrina, who owned Best Friend's Boutique and had eagerly spread the word about Amanda's mobile dog grooming services.

Amanda glanced out the window. It had been dark when she had arrived for the emergency grooming visit. Now, beams of light were breaking through the morning fog and giving everything a soft glow.

Just a few months earlier, Amanda had left Ohio's overcast skies and her unfaithful ex, driving her grooming RV westward with the hopes of a fresh start and a reunion with her estranged twin, Alexandra. She arrived in Ocean Wood on California's Central Coast to find her sister missing and a dead body in her house. The murder had been solved, but not the mystery of her sister's disappearance.

Amanda's grooming RV was parked on the steep road next to Katrina's shop, the vehicle a stark contrast to the elegant Victorian house turned business. Ocean Wood's residential area had many historic homes but the houses closer to the town center had been converted to shops that sidled up to larger two-story retail buildings. The street she was parked on led to the ocean, and between houses, you could catch glimpses of the cerulean blue water.

"I was right."

At the sound of a voice coming from the door, Amanda squeaked and jumped, banging her head on the cabinet above the table.

Buddy waved his tail in welcome, his now clean, silky golden hair fanning her arm.

Amanda put a hand to her heart. "Grok, I've asked you not to sneak up on me." Then she reached up and rubbed her head, ruffling the messy bun of copper-colored frizzy hair.

"Who's sneaking? The kids in the annual butterfly parade could have screamed down the street and you wouldn't have heard over the racket you were making."

Amanda refused to acknowledge he was right and instead glared at the thirty-five-pound Maine Coon cat in the doorway. "And what if Katrina was in here? What would she have thought of us talking to each other?"

When Grok had first explained to Amanda that she and Alexandra were the only ones who could understand him and everyone else just heard "meows," she didn't believe him. But it was true. For some reason, people around town gave him unparalleled access to their shops, restaurants, and homes but still treated him like an ordinary, albeit nosy, cat. They never hinted they could understand him.

The cat scoffed. "How do humans explain any of the strange things they do?" He stalked over to a bed Amanda had placed in the corner for him and sprawled across it and over the sides. "Your species is a conundrum of odd behavior."

Amanda thought that was rich, coming from a psychic, amnesiac cat who couldn't remember who he was or where he was from but had definite ideas on human behavior. All the same, he was a very clever cat. "So, someone was there. Did you recognize them?"

"No." The cat stretched out a hind paw and groomed between his toes.

"You about done there? He looks beautiful," Katrina said from the door.

Amanda jumped and hit her head again. Was it too early in the morning to have a heart attack? She motioned for Katrina to come inside while she recovered. "All done. I'd keep him on his leash so you don't have a repeat before you can make it out of town."

Amanda helped Buddy off the table and started sweeping up the clouds of hair. Katrina sniffed Buddy's fur, and a dreamy look washed over her face.

Amanda smiled. She got caught sniffing her client's pets all the time. "Nothing smells as good as a freshly washed and dried dog,"

"Agreed!" Katrina pulled out her wallet. "What are your plans now? You seem to be settling into your sister's house."

"Oh, I'm only staying until she comes back. It feels strange being there while she's gone."

"Would you leave town?"

Amanda's hand stilled as she reached for the card. She hadn't thought about what she would do when Alexandra returned. It would depend on whether her sister would forgive her, and then they could get to know each other again. But the idea leaving town when she had just started over again left an ache in her chest. "Not sure what will happen when Alexandra comes back. Have to find her first."

They completed the transaction, and Katrina returned her wallet to her purse. "Well, thank you for squeezing us in. You're a lifesaver. Oh, if you see a certain detective, tell him I'll be back on Monday." She wiggled her eyebrows.

"Why would I see a detective?" Amanda certainly hoped she wouldn't have a run-in with any of the members of the Ocean Wood Police Department anytime soon.

"Oh, you know, if you bump into him with your geeky-hot medical examiner friend."

Before Amanda could sputter a protest that she thought of her friend Ben as geeky, or hot, even though, objectively he was both of those, Katrina winked. She snapped on the lead and exited the van with Buddy following close behind, the Golden Retriever's tail waving like a happy flag.

Amanda was securing her equipment to drive when her phone rang, and she fumbled the device out of her pocket, almost dropping it in her haste. Technically, it wasn't opening hours yet and she should send it to voicemail, but she wasn't in a position to turn down work.

"Good morning. Pink Power Wash and Groom. How —" She was cut off.

"Amanda? I need your help." A loud machine noise in the background almost drowned out the voice, but it couldn't block the sounds of barking dogs and a woman shouting.

"Ben?"

"Yes, please, come to the marina. It's Qbert—Oh no. Quick, get a bucket." Ben was talking to someone else at the same time, but the call cut off before she could find out what was happening.

"We have to go; Ben needs my help," she told Grok as she quickly finished securing the grooming area for travel.

Grok stopped licking and glared at her. "But we haven't had breakfast. You promised after this emergency appointment we would eat."

"I know. I'm sorry, but Ben needs us. I'll get you something there," Amanda said, trying to bribe the cat, even knowing she would have to live with the consequences if she couldn't fulfill the promise. "If you want to sit up front, you need to hurry up."

"You hurry. I'm suffering in silence, starved and neglected."

Amanda rolled her eyes.

She locked the side door, and when she opened the cab access door, Grok slipped through. As she settled into the driver's seat and put the key in the ignition, she caught her image in the mirror; pale skin and freckles topped with coppery hair flying around her face. Amanda quickly pulled her hair out of the bun and into a ponytail.

Grok groaned as he settled into the passenger seat next to her. "Your terrible fur can wait. My stomach can't!"

Despite his attitude, the cat had taken on a sort of guardianship of her, dogging her steps and tracking her moves. Amanda couldn't say she hated it. It was nice to have him around, and if he was fed regularly, he didn't turn on his gremlin-like attitude.

"I wonder what's happening on Ben's new boat." Ben was her first friend, and his dog, Qbert, was her first client in town. Even now, when his work at Ocean Wood's small medical examiner's office got busy, he would call her to help out with the dog.

She turned the key in the ignition. The starter whined and died.

The Pink Pup was her pride and joy. Okay, she would admit that the whole-body wrap that made the van look like a giant pink dog, especially the huge faux fur ears, was a little unusual. It hadn't helped when, a few weeks ago, a murderous neighbor tried to light the van on fire, singeing the ears and leaving the RV looking like a burnt pink marshmallow.

She tried the starter again, vowing that if the Pink Pup didn't fail her, she would trade services with her mechanic client and get a tune-up.

The engine stuttered then started. Amanda blew out a breath of relief. Maybe she could put off a tune-up a little longer.

THREE

Rude Awakening

Amanda arrived in the marina's parking lot before the Pink Pup stalled.

"If I had hands, I would clap," Grok said from the passenger seat.

She shot him a glare as she unbuckled her seat belt. "Not helping. We need to hurry. I don't know what is wrong, but Ben sounded frantic." She grabbed her purse from between the seats and slid out the driver's door, holding it open for the cat.

This was Amanda's first visit to Ocean Wood Harbor Marina. The parking lot faced a large building connected to a tall, chain link fence that protected row after row of docks locked together like puzzle pieces. Boats bobbed in the water, most shrouded with covers, sails wrapped, and curtains zipped tight. Looking around the sea of vinyl mounds with tall masts, she scanned for Ben. There was a commotion way in the back, in the last dock before open water.

"Come on, Grok. Let's see if that's him."

The marina gate was locked. Amanda jiggled the knob then pulled out her phone and called Ben. He didn't answer.

"Move aside," said a voice behind Amanda.

She turned to see a beautiful blonde woman holding a pair of red-sable Pekingese with long, flowing hair.

Amanda moved off to the side, and the woman stepped forward and waited.

"Excuse me." The deep voice came from behind Amanda. She stepped back farther, and a tall, dignified man in his early sixties reached around the woman and punched in a gate code. The blonde woman with the dogs swept through the gate in a cloud of perfume.

Amanda called after her. "Your Pekingese are beautiful."

The woman didn't stop. Just as the gate was closing, Grok jumped over the threshold and stopped it.

"Well, what are you waiting for?" Grok followed the question with a low rumbling of annoyance.

"We can't go in there; we need permission from the marina, or a captain, or whatever they do on a boat," Amanda hissed at the cat, forgetting the tall man still standing just inside the gate.

"Are you talking to me?" The man's frown disappeared in his close-cropped white beard.

"No? No," Amanda stammered, unnerved by how put together he looked with his crisp white uniform and sparkling teeth. "I'm looking for my friend. He told us to meet him at the marina."

He smiled at her embarrassment. "Does he have a boat docked here?"

"Yes. He just got moved in yesterday." Amanda angled her neck to look deeper into the boatyard.

"Well, let's see if we can find him." The man in the starched white uniform pushed the door open and indicated Amanda should proceed with him. "Do you know where his slip is?"

She hadn't thought there would be so many boats. If Ben wasn't answering his phone, how would she ever find him? Amanda shook her head.

"Hey, you can't be in here." Several docks away, an older man in khaki pants called across the water at Amanda and Grok. He had his hands on his hips and glared as if the sheer force of his disapproval would propel them out of the marina.

"It's okay, Jack. They're with me." The man they were following backtracked so he was visible around the hull of an equally blindingly white boat.

"Oh, skipper, didn't see you there." The khaki pants man immediately relaxed.

"Glad to know you are keeping things safe." The skipper winked.

"It's a never-ending job. Thieves have been stealing our equipment. Our newest liveaboard is taking on water, and I'm trying to find our diver, Tobias. Have you seen him?" Jack scratched his bald head.

"No, I don't believe I've met him. But this lady is looking for her friend Ben. Could that be the new resident?"

"Yep, that's him. He's in that wreck tied up next to your vessel." The man pointed to the far end of the marina, closest to the open bay, then strode off muttering, "I never should have approved that sale."

"Sounds like your friend might be in a bit of trouble. Follow me." The man in white pointed to a dock that branched off to the left.

"That was the marina manager, Jack Roberts, an old landlocked sea dog. My name is Captain Jeffrey Cook. Watch your footing here." Jeffrey pointed to a tricky section of the dock with multiple obstacles.

A real captain! Amanda was so excited she almost forgot to introduce herself. "I'm Amanda Warren, and my cat's name is Grok."

"He's not afraid of the water?" Jeffrey studied the large Maine Coon striding confidently beside them.

"No, he recently discovered he loves swimming."

"Huh. An odd name for an odd cat."

The statement triggered Grok's warning growl, and Amanda quickly changed the subject. "What are you the captain of? Do you live in Monterey?"

He shook his head. "I'm the captain of the *Moonstone* out of San Diego."

"You own the boat?"

The skipper chuckled. "No, the owners are Alan and Luna Erling."

"But Jack knows you?"

They had reached another branch in the dock, and Jeffrey held an arm out to the right. "We're here a couple of times a year."

As they turned the corner, Amanda could see where the commotion was coming from. Up ahead, a wooden boat was dwarfed by the enormous yacht docked beside it. The dock around the wooden boat was littered with equipment, and several pumps were pouring water over the hull out into the marina.

Her friend, Ben, and a woman she didn't recognize were coming up from below deck on the smaller boat. Amanda hurried up to the normally impeccably put together dark-haired man and took in his rumpled appearance. "What happened?"

Ben was startled when he saw her. "Oh, thank goodness. I'm so glad to see you. Qbert has been a mess."

A dog barked a greeting, and Amanda turned to the sound. Several feet away, tied to a cleat on the dock, a large sheepdog was wearing a neon green life vest.

"The boat was fine when I bought it last week. I rechecked it when I moved in yesterday. But in the middle of the night, Qbert started barking. It woke me up, and I discovered we were taking on water. I've been bailing for hours. Mo turned up early this morning and showed me how to use the bilge and crash pumps. She's the marina mechanic." Ben indicated the woman in overalls next to him.

Amanda greeted the woman then turned back to Ben. "This is awful. Are you okay?"

"Yeah, most of my stuff is still in the car. I just had to get Qbert and me out when it started sinking. We've got enough water pumped out that we can look at the inside of the hull now." Under his breath, Ben whispered, "My bargain boat might have been too good to be true."

"Nonsense," bellowed the woman next to them. Her volume was out of sync with the noise around them. "All boats take maintenance. Old boats take more. This old girl's got a lot of life left in her. Someone's just been using her and not caring for her. We'll get her out of the water and sealed up. She'll be a gem again with a little sealant, an engine tune-up, and maybe a coat of varnish. You'll see." The woman whacked Ben on the shoulders, almost propelling him into the water.

Qbert barked. From somewhere, another dog yipped a response.

Grok whined. "We aren't going to be getting breakfast here either, are we?"

Amanda was the only one who could understand the cat, so she ignored him and turned back to Ben. "How can I help?"

Grok let out a disgusted sound and, with a swish of his fluffy tail, left.

A voice above them shouted, "Will someone shut that dog up? It's upsetting Daisy and Poppy."

The woman Amanda had met earlier at the gate looked down on them from the second story of the yacht.

Ben waved a frantic hand between the woman and Qbert, who was keeping up a steady stream of barking. To Amanda he said, "He won't stop, and I can't put him back on the boat or leave him in the car. I've not got time to walk him now with this going on. I've got to call into work and tell them I've had an emergency. Can you take Qbert for the day?"

"Of course. I'll get him now, and he can travel with me to my appointments. Just call when you want him back."

Ben sagged with relief. "Thank you."

"The water's slowing down. Let's check what's visible in the hull. We might get lucky and see where it's leaking." Mo climbed back onto the boat, and Ben followed.

Amanda turned toward the dog, who was barking and scratching at the dock between the two boats. "All right, Mr. Qbert, what a rough morning you've had. How about we take you on a walk?" Amanda had taken care of Qbert before, and usually he lost his mind when offered a walk, but he ignored her and continued to bark and scratch at the dock. His lead pulled tight as he leaned over the side, his nose pointing into the dark water. Amanda crouched beside the dog and ran a soothing hand down his back. This wasn't like him.

"What did you find?" Following the animal's gaze, Amanda was unable to see more than a couple of inches into the dark water. "Did you see a fish?"

Qbert gave a whine and dropped to his belly, paws curling over the edge of the dock as he stared intently into the darkness.

"Come on, boy, let's walk." She tried again, pulling on the leash.

Qbert refused to rise, inching his way closer to the edge, his nose dropping lower.

Amanda dropped to her knees and pulled on the back of the vest to keep the dog back, but Qbert didn't care. He looked up and gave an excited yelp before turning back and grabbing at something under the edge of the dock.

"Did you find a stick?" Amanda didn't like the idea of him playing with a slimy, waterlogged piece of wood, but if it would keep him from barking, it would be worth it.

Qbert tugged, but his prize seemed caught on something. Amanda leaned over to help him. What was that? The white object Qbert had pulled free from under the dock bobbed in the water.

That looks like a hand...

Before Amanda could finish the thought, a dark object attached to the white thing broke free from under the dock. With the ebb and flow of the water, the object turned and slowly rose.

Amanda screamed as a body floated to the surface, a large bolt sticking from its chest.

FOUR

Bailing

The morning sun bathed the area in gentle light as Amanda stood next to Ben on the dock. She grabbed his hand and squeezed as she watched the dripping body emerge from the dark water. Excluding the mottled face and pruny white hands, it looked like a candle dipped in black wax.

Qbert lunged forward, tail wagging, excited to meet the new friend he had found. Ben grabbed for the collar and, kneeling, looped an arm over the dog's life jacket, holding him back as they watched the police pull the body from the water and gently lower it to the deck. Officer Hartman wore gloves as he turned the body to lie on its back, the short spear through its chest sticking out at an angle.

Out of the water, she could see it was a diver in a black wetsuit with a yellow stripe running down the side. The face looked young, too young. Amanda swayed, tipping precariously close to the water at the side of the dock.

"Come here." Ben pulled her by the waist to sit next to him.

Amanda stifled a cough and tried not to gag as she turned her face into Ben's shoulder and breathed in the scent of stale ocean water and engine grease. That was worse. She whipped her head back but kept facing away from the scene.

"Sorry. I haven't had a chance to shower." Frustration vibrated in Ben's voice.

"Can I leave?" Amanda's voice sounded faint.

"Not yet. You need to talk to the detective when he arrives. I've got a few things I need to say to him too."

The patrol officer who arrived first had been new. It was his first homicide, and he was relieved to see Ben had confirmed the diver was dead and secured the body so it didn't float away. When they couldn't find the marina manager, Ben helped the officer hunt down a winch and set up the extraction. Before they could start, Officer Hartman arrived and, puffing up his mustache, claimed authority over the site, as neither an ambulance nor the crime scene unit had been called yet. He used a rule Amanda had never heard of to ban Ben from going near the body.

"You can look. They've got him out now and under a — Hey, do not touch that spear." Ben moved Amanda's hand to Qbert's life vest and shot to his feet.

Amanda stretched her neck to look up at Ben as he glared at the officer.

"You're keeping me from doing my job as Chief

Medical Examiner for Monterey," Ben reminded the officer—and everyone at the marina.

Officer Hartman didn't like Amanda and Grok, who called him the "hairy-lipped male." But she hadn't realized his dislike extended to Ben.

A crowd had gathered at the fence, peering down at the marina like they were staring into a fishbowl. They parted, and an officer hurried over to open the marina gate. A tall man in an impeccable suit with short, dark hair strode down the dock towards them. Detective Kim paused to say something to the officer at the gate, who straightened his spine to attention. The detective continued across the marina, stopping for a report when he got to Officer Hartman.

As they talked, the detective's keen eyes assessed the scene. Even several boat slips away, Amanda could see his brows shoot up when the officer pointed to Amanda and Ben. Detective Kim acknowledged the report and moved towards them. "So, here we are again."

Amanda opened her mouth to speak, but Ben burst out first. "That...that...officer is obstructing an investigation. Can you believe he told me he would arrest me if I touched the deceased? That is literally my job!" Ben sputtered through the question and flung his arms wide.

Startled, Qbert jumped sideways. The dog scuttered back when he almost landed in the water, and there was an awkward moment when everyone reshuffled their position on the narrow dock.

"So, you were the first on the scene?" Detective Kim's face was unreadable as he consulted his notebook.

"Well, no. I was already here. That is my boat." Ben pointed back towards the grisly scene.

The detective's brow creased. "Did you sleep here last night?"

"I wouldn't say I got much sleep." Ben shook his head, and his short, dark curls bounced. "It was a hard night for a variety of reasons. Qbert was restless, and he woke me up barking several times. A little after two a.m., I finally got up to take him on a walk. That's when I realized the floor was damp. He probably saved the boat. I've been bailing nonstop ever since. Mo, the marina mechanic"—he nodded towards the woman in stained overalls still on his boat—"got in about six and showed me how to use the bilge pumps. Once the water started going down, I called Amanda for help with Qbert."

"So, you discovered the body?"

A disruption from the gate snagged Amanda's attention. She stood and watched with the others as Ben's transport team arrived. They struggled with the gurney as the wheels clattered against the boards of the plastic dock.

As Ben surged towards them, the detective held up a hand to block him while waiting for Ben's answer.

"Uh, no. That was Amanda and Qbert—you know, I really need to help them out."

The detective sighed. "No, you don't. Sorry, Ben, but we need to understand the timeframe better before I can clear your involvement."

Ben sputtered.

The detective shook his head. "Let me check with the

chief and your supervisor before you look at the body. Hands off until then."

Ben's shoulders dropped. "I'm a suspect."

Detective Kim cringed. "I didn't say that. I'll let you know what happens."

There was more noise at the scene, but Amanda couldn't see what was happening as Detective Kim had turned his attention to her and asked, "So, you found the body?"

"Really? Again?" The noise of the scene dropped as the voice broke across the water.

Amanda groaned. It was her biggest skeptic, Chief of Police Gina Rodriguez.

The chief was her twin sister's best friend and former police partner. Amanda had heard the duo stayed close after Alexandra left the force to become a private investigator. Then, just a few weeks ago, Alexandra disappeared, and Amanda had arrived just as a body turned up in her sister's house. Sure, they had resolved that neither she nor her twin had anything to do with that body, but here she was again when someone was killed.

As the chief made her way towards them, her laser glare almost cut Amanda in half. "How is it that you have discovered another body?"

"Wasn't me," Amanda choked out.

"It wasn't?" Detective Kim raised a brow as he glanced between her and Ben.

"No. Qbert found the body." Amanda pointed to the dog at her feet.

Qbert stood up and gave an excited wag of his tail as everyone looked down at him.

Amanda explained how the dog had alerted her to something in the water. She shivered as she relayed the rest of the events. "So, Ben couldn't have been involved in whatever happened. He was busy with Mo."

"Amanda, the body has been in the water for hours. This didn't just happen." Ben nudged Qbert with his knee as the dog licked Detective Kim's shoe.

"Huh. I wonder if it's Tobias?" Amanda immediately regretted saying that aloud.

"Ah-ha!" Chief Rodriguez stuck a finger in Amanda's face.

Amanda reeled back, and Ben grabbed her arm to help her balance.

Qbert, in the center of the group, saw this as an opportunity to explore and stuck his face in the crotch of the woman leaning over him.

Chief Rodriguez shouted and stepped back. Her foot hovered over the edge of the dock, finding no purchase. All of them lunged for the officer.

Ben tripped over Qbert.

Detective Kim's notebook flew into the air as he spun and twisted up his legs, unable to grab his boss.

Amanda's fingers grasped at the woman's black uniform tie. Metal stars ripped from her collar and sailed by the chief's bulging face as the tie tightened.

The sound of choking and the chief's hand smacking Amanda's away was followed by a loud splash.

FIVE

Slippery

Trapped near the end of one of the fingers of the dock that jutted out into the water, Amanda tried to make herself as small as possible and stay out of everyone's way.

It didn't take long to get the chief out of the water, and as she left the marina to be driven home, the scene went back to investigation mode. Detective Kim and Ben returned to Amanda, both still wearing stunned expressions.

"Is she okay?"

"She wasn't hurt but has a very bruised pride."

"I wish she didn't hate me," Amanda muttered, not needing to say who she was talking about.

A ghost of a smile crossed the detective's face before it disappeared. "I'd stay away for a while. For the record, I don't think she hates you as much as she dislikes the memories you evoke."

That didn't make Amanda feel any better.

"Okay." The detective blew out a breath. "Let's try this again. So, how do you know the victim?"

"I don't. This is my first time here. This guy, a captain or something, helped me get access to the marina this morning. The marina manager stopped us and said he was looking for a diver named Tobias."

"Did he say when he last saw him?"

Amanda shook her head. "That's all I know. Who is this Tobias, and how did he get shot?"

Detective Kim ignored her question and, checking his notebook, turned to Ben. "I talked to your mechanic, Mo. She's got an alibi. She was home with her husband last night. But you don't have an alibi before six a.m. Did anyone see you?"

"Well, if they did, they didn't offer to help." Ben threw his hands up then winced and rubbed his triceps.

"How many people live here at the marina?" The detective scanned the marina, taking in the gentle bobbing of the boats covered in canvas. It looked like they were snoring softly as they slept into the day.

"A fair amount. I've met five, no six liveaboards, but I know there are more, maybe fifteen." Ben followed the detective's gaze.

The detective furrowed his brow. "What is a liveaboard?"

"People who live on their boats at the marina full time." Ben pointed to a few boats that had more obvious signs of occupancy.

"Well, most of the liveaboards, as you called them, that I've talked to are couples who vouched for each other, though I'm just getting started. I'd really like to question the people staying on that big yacht." Detective Kim pointed up to the boat that loomed over Ben's and had a good view of the marina.

"The marina manager, Jack Roberts, will have their contact information. You'll want to talk to him anyway since he's a liveaboard, too. He sleeps in the club sometimes, though I don't know why when his boat is just a few yards away." Ben shrugged.

There was a commotion on the dock as someone struggled to get through the crowd. A man with a beet-red face fought his way through and demanded to know what was happening.

"That's him. That's the manager." Amanda pointed to the man.

"I better go take care of this and try and find a witness who actually saw something." The detective gave Qbert a pat on the head, and then he stood up and headed towards the crowd.

"Hey, boss. We got a preliminary report for you." A man in a full protective suit—Ben had told her they sometimes called them bunny suits—walked over to them. Ben held up a hand to stop him, but the man didn't see it; his white Tyveks-covered head was bent over a clipboard, and he spoke in a rote voice as he read aloud. "The cause of death appears to be a spear gun bolt to the chest, which likely resulted in instantaneous death. There aren't any apparent superficial injuries. The preliminary time of death is challenging due to cold-water conditions. It's likely the body's been submerged for an extended period, possibly through the night. A more accurate determination will be possible after conducting further examinations at the medical office." The man looked up. "How was that?"

Ben's lips tightened into a grim smile. "That was good, Andrew, but I've not been cleared to work the case yet. You have to go tell the detective."

The man's face fell. "Oh, sure. Where is he?"

"Come on, I'll show you. Hey, why is Officer Hartman on my boat?"

"Said he was checking for evidence."

"Really? We will just see about that."

Ben marched up the dock.

Amanda wondered if she could slip away now that she had answered the detective's questions. But they hadn't told her she could go, and she still had to watch Qbert. She could take the dog with her, but what if Ben wanted both of them there for support?

A voice behind her in the water asked, "Excuse me. What's happening?"

Startled, Amanda stepped forward and turned to see a tall, fit woman jumping off a paddle board onto the dock. "You surprised me!"

"Sorry." The tall, tanned woman was covered in freckles, her sandy blonde hair woven into a French braid. She stooped to pull the paddle board onto the dock.

Amanda put a hand on the boat beside her for balance.

The boat gently moved away from the touch. Unsteady, she blurted out, "Someone died, and it wasn't an accident."

Amanda immediately felt bad; she had been thinking that, but it wasn't something she should have said.

"What?" The blonde woman dropped the paddle boat and rushed past Amanda, stopping when she saw the body. A look of horror crossed her face. "Tobias?"

Amanda put her hand on the woman's arm as she wobbled. "Did you know him?"

A minute of stunned silence followed the question. The woman choked out a sob and whispered, "No." After clearing her throat, her voice was shaky as she replied, "Yes, we worked together. I can't—how? What happened?"

"We don't know. We just found him. Do you want to sit down?" Amanda pointed to the storage box. She received a blank-eyed stare, and Amanda guided the woman over until she collapsed onto the box, her head and arms sinking between her legs.

Amanda sat beside her as she sobbed, noting her bare feet. As the sobs ended, the woman started to shiver. She had dropped a bag on the deck when she jumped off the paddle board, and Amanda wondered if she should look inside it for a sweater or shoes.

"What is going on here?"

Amanda recognized the detective's voice and appreciated the soft tone he used. She stood and let the detective take her place.

"What's your name?" His voice was gentle.

The blonde lifted her head and pushed herself up with her hands on her knees. "Robin—Robin McArthur."

The detective nodded. "Do you know the young man?"

"Yes. Its Tobias, Tobias Grant. We work—we worked together here. He helps with maintenance and odd jobs." Hair hung in the woman's face; her red-rimmed eyes were drawn back to the area where the body was being loaded onto the medical examiner's gurney.

"And what do you do at the marina, Robin?"

The woman closed her eyes and blew out a breath, and then she opened her eyes and pushed to stand on shaky legs. "Sorry, it's a shock. I'm the marina's sailing instructor. Tobias helps—helped me with classes and boat mainte-nance sometimes, though most of his work was with Mo. She's our mechanic."

"When was the last time you saw him?" the detective asked.

Amanda's ears perked up.

Ben headed their way, and she raised a finger to stall him, wanting to hear the blonde's answer before they were interrupted.

"Last night sometime? I don't know. I had an evening cruise. He was here when I returned, having words with the new guy, and then he helped me put away the boat."

"The new guy?"

Robin pointed to Ben.

Detective Kim made a note before adding, "How did Tobias seem?"

"Fine. Impatient, a little annoyed... It had been a long day."

"You both live here?"

"Yes, which means we're pretty much on call 24/7. I have a sailboat I offer charters on, and Tobias had an old yacht, almost in as bad of shape as that one." She nodded in the direction of Ben's boat.

"Are you a diver too?"

"I'm a sailor," she answered quickly. "I like being on the water, not in it. Is that all? I need to go check in with Jack."

The detective seemed satisfied for the moment, and he released her to leave with a warning. "Stay in town. I'll have more questions."

The woman gave an abrupt nod and headed towards the marina manager, passing Ben on the way.

"They wouldn't let me on my boat. Officer Hartman is treating it like the crime scene. Is this your doing, Kim?" Ben looked flustered; his hands were wet, and he seemed concerned about where to dry them. Finally, he wiped them on his pants, amplifying his uncharacteristic, disheveled appearance.

"Ben, did you know the deceased?"

"No, I don't think so, I just moved in. About my boat—"

Detective Kim interrupted, "You were seen arguing with him last evening."

Ben's face dropped. "I was? I don't remember him. It was a little chaotic when I was moving in."

Officer Hartman walked up the dock behind Ben, a

smug smile on his face and an evidence bag in his hand. "Found this."

Detective Kim reached out and accepted the bag, studying the contents. Then he held it up for them to see. "Want to explain to me why you had a diver's glove in your bedroom?"

Ben's mouth flapped like a fish gasping for water. He finally caught his breath. "I've never seen that before in my life."

The detective shook his head. "I'm sorry, Ben, I can't let you near this case. If we handle this wrong, it could professionally discredit you and impact all the other cases you've worked on."

Ben swallowed hard but refused to break eye contact with the detective. "I'm not involved. I don't know how that glove ended up on my boat."

The detective nodded, face grim. "I'm going to let the chief know. She'll contact your boss. I expect she will call you once she is dry and back in the office.

Ben scrubbed a hand over his face then gave a curt nod of acknowledgment.

As the detective turned to leave, Amanda remembered the message she was supposed to deliver. "Detective? Katrina wanted me to let you know she will return Monday."

Detective Kim had turned around to hear the message so Amanda could see the blush that started at his neck and worked its way up.

"I, um, don't know why she'd want me, uh, to

know that. But thanks for delivering, or rather, letting me know." Kim spun back and quickly walked away.

Ben shook his head. "That was strange. Nothing rattles that man."

Amanda was going to respond, but Qbert decided he'd done enough waiting. His leash slipped through Amanda's hands, and the dog took off.

"Don't worry, I got this," Amanda called to Ben over her shoulder as she raced after Qbert.

SIX

Overboard

Grok's stomach growled, and he echoed the sound in his throat. His patience was wearing thin. He wiggled his nose as he padded alongside Amanda. He didn't smell anything worthy of his palate here. The marina stunk of stale water, brine, and gasoline. Or maybe that was just Amanda's friend, Ben. The normally impeccably groomed man could use a bath, like his dog Qbert, who was bouncing around on a too-short leash that kept snapping him back.

Grok was rather proud of his sense of smell, more so than even his dry wit, which Amanda had come to treasure in him. He even had a scent organ in the roof of his mouth that helped him detect people and objects. That is why he smelled the body before he saw it stuck under the edge of the dock. Though, technically Qbert found it, if he could get anyone to pay attention to his proud howls of discovery.

The dog had no idea what it meant. Grok knew from

his experience as an investigator that it doomed them to another long delay between him and food.

Hmm. When was he an investigator?

With no hope of redeeming his morning, Grok decided he might as well find a place out of the way to ride out the next couple of hours. He considered telling Amanda about the body, but just yesterday she had accused him of being a chatterbox. Which had hurt. If Amanda had only one person who she could give orders to, he imagined she would be rather chatty too. And that dopey dog looked so pleased with himself. Might as well let him take the credit. Without a backward glance, Grok left the humans behind and retreated from the scene for higher ground.

He found a sweet spot on the canvas-covered upper deck of a boat vehicle on the other side of the marina. It was close enough to see what was coming but should be quiet enough for a nap. Amanda truly had no idea what he put up with. He should make a list of grievances and helpful suggestions of what she could do better. She would appreciate that.

It didn't take long for the action to start. Amanda shouted for Ben, and everyone in the area rushed to see what was going on.

While the humans watched the grisly discovery, Grok watched them.

Ben arrived first, along with the greasy woman helping him with his boat. The male leaned over the water and felt for a pulse. The shake of his head stopped the woman from jumping in.

Grok could have told them the body was way past saving and several hours dead if his nose was right.

Someone said it was a "diver," which must have something to do with his black suit.

Grok's attention wandered as the humans below talked and talked but did little. Most of the boat vehicles bobbing in the water were wrapped up and closed off, empty, silent hulls except for the constant chiming from their tall sticks. A few of these boats had people living on them. As the talking got louder, they emerged, and Grok studied them but ultimately dismissed them as being of little interest.

When the police finally arrived, they started working to retrieve the body. The next group to arrive was the team that worked with Ben, followed immediately by the detective and Grok's old nemesis, Rodriguez.

The chief didn't like him any more than he liked her. When Amanda's sister, Alexandra, was here, the police officer had watched him with narrowed eyes. She was smart for a human. Even Grok didn't know who he was, good or bad, but he knew he was more than just a cat and he knew there was something dangerous about his situation. Any attempt to access his memory had resulted in disaster, but still the thought dangled in the back of his mind like a piece of yarn begging to be snagged.

The nosy man—Jack—who'd yelled at them earlier came running from the other side of the marina. He pushed through the small crowd, forcing his way to the front, and demanded answers from the hairy-lipped male. Grok whined. He would keep an eye on both those males.

Behind Amanda, a woman stepped from the water like magic then almost collapsed on the deck minutes later. Grok narrowed his eyes at the overwrought display. That woman was another one to watch.

He scanned the crowd neatly contained within the marina's fencing and confined to the floating docks. Something was missing.

A small dog barked. The sound came from the largest boat in the marina. Parked next to Ben's vessel, the multi-level house on water cast a shadow over the proceedings. Only, no one came out to look.

A movement on the top deck caught his eye. It was the pair of Pekingese. They bounced up and down on a long sun bed on the boat's bow. There was no way the small dogs could see the commotion below from that vantage point. But they must have heard Qbert's bark.

Grok caught another movement. Tucked into the shadows on the top deck, a blonde woman and man embraced. He couldn't see if it was the rude woman from the gate. Where was the old man in white?

Surely, the police arriving and all the associated noise would have brought everyone on that boat to the railing to see what was happening.

Bored of watching, Grok rolled onto his back and stared up at the blue sky as his mind worked the scene over in his head. Amanda seemed as eager to involve herself in these situations as her sister had been. Sure, she protested more, but even without the training, she was just as curious and astute as her twin. She would undoubtedly listen in on the tidbits from the police as to how and when someone killed the human, and he knew she would find his observations most interesting. He rolled to the other side, and the cloth beneath him shifted.

Grok cursed. He had miscalculated his position.

With nothing in the slick material to gain traction from and stop his decline, he lost control and slid from the high vantage point to a lower deck, his fur hastening his slide.

Grok blasted right to the edge of the wire railing on the lower deck and would have dropped if the claw of his right paw hadn't snagged the material at the last minute. Hind legs hanging free, he scrambled for purchase on the smooth hull of the boat.

As Grok dangled from the one paw, a notion went through his mind. In his previous life as an expert security officer, he would never have let such a stupid mistake occur. Others had depended on his cunning and knowledge. The thought was still fresh in his mind, as the blinding pain that followed any attempt to access his memories from his time before Earth pierced through his head. He growled as his mind fuzzed over, and he lost consciousness before hitting the water.

SEVEN

Wet Cat

Amanda raced across the marina to the far corner, farthest from the shore and several rows from the crime scene. She caught up with Qbert in time to hear a low growl of irritation she'd come to think of as Grok's trademark noise. A splash followed. She hurried down the dock, following the dog.

"Qbert, where is he?" Stumbling, she tripped over a cleat hitch sticking up from the dock.

Qbert barked louder and more insistent than he had at the body. He was dragging his leash, snagging it on hitches and ropes as he ran. Amanda took a second to unclip the lead. The dog dashed down the dock towards a big boat wrapped in blue canvas like a present. Following, she arrived in time to grab his collar before he dove into the water. There, floating in the slip next to the boat, was a gray fur rug that Amanda knew was Grok.

She dropped to the dock and, ignoring the pain in her knees, leaned forward and wrapped a hand around the rope of a fender dangling from the boat. She reached into the water and grabbed the cat, catching him under his belly and pulling. He was heavy. She tightened her grip and grunted as she pulled him up. The unexpected weight caused the boat to sway. Bracing herself as she dangled over the water, clutching the enormous, waterlogged cat to her chest, she waited for the vessel to sway back so she could leverage herself onto the dock. She had just about resigned herself to the bath when she felt a hand at her waistband.

"Hold on, Amanda, Grok. We have you."

Ben's voice sent a wave of relief through her. An arm slipped under her belly, and she was yanked back from the brink, pulling Grok with her.

Collapsed on the dock with the wet cat sprawled across her face and chest, Amanda's choked in breath of air had her smelling the cat's new aroma of rotten eggs mixed with decaying matter. She gagged.

"What happened?" Ben asked, panting from his sprint.

"He must have fallen in." She didn't mention that the cat frequently lost consciousness. How could she? Ben didn't know that Grok was an amnesiac psychic cat who could speak to her and passed out whenever he tried to recall anything from his past. Hopefully, Ben would never find out.

"But why isn't he moving?"

Amanda rolled out from under Grok and got to her knees. *Oh no!*

"Grok? Wake up!" She shook the cat's shoulders gently, then harder, pulling him into her lap. Was he breathing? Could you give mouth-to-mouth to a cat?

Qbert started licking Grok's face.

"He's waking up." Ben pointed to the cat.

Amanda pushed Qbert out of the way. Grok's eyes were open but unfocused as he slid off her lap to lie on the deck, his head swaying. He was breathing now and even sputtering and hissing at Qbert to back off.

Amanda slumped beside the cat. "Thank goodness you reeled us in."

"I heard Qbert going crazy. Twice, he came to the rescue today." Ben patted the big sheepdog's head and scratched behind his ears.

Amanda pulled her phone out of her pocket, relieved for a second time that she hadn't just taken a bath in the bay. "Grok, I'm going to call the vet and let him know I'm bringing you in."

Ben tilted his head and looked at Amanda with a frown. He used a hand to push back the big, black-framed glasses that had slipped down his nose. "Are you asking his permission?"

Before Amanda could cover up her mistake, Grok gave a low, rumbling growl of disproval and struggled slowly to his paws.

"No doctors," the cat hissed as he started moving.

Ben and Amanda scrambled to follow.

Ben walked with Amanda as she led a slowly weaving Grok to the marina gate. The cat refused to be carried.

"Are you really off this case? Who will do the autopsy?" Amanda held the gate for the animals.

"They'll probably send the body to Salinas. It's okay. I've got to figure out what is going on with my boat. I..."

Ben paused and looked around, blinking his eyes. "I might have undersold how bad last night was. I got seasick, and Qbert kept waking me up. He was chasing a mouse, following it around the boat, barking. He dropped it on my head while I was sleeping. I flung it across the room but was too sick to get out of bed. And then he got so loud, I finally forced myself up and found out we were taking on water. Mo says the repairs may be expensive. I might have made a mistake buying a boat." Ben bit his lip, his face earnest and shoulders slumped.

"I think your celebration dinner tonight might be premature. What if I tell everyone we're just going to the pub?"

Ben's eyes bulged. "I completely forgot."

"Don't worry. I'll let the others know." As Amanda reached out to pat his arm, she heard a shout from the back of the clubhouse. She turned toward the sound just in time to see Robin shout and shove a man against the wall. They were in shadow, and she couldn't see who the sailing instructor was arguing with.

She moved towards them but the two people disappeared around the corner of the clubhouse.

"What do you think that was about?" Amanda turned back to Ben, who shook his head.

As she left Ben behind, she felt she had started her day with too much excitement and not nearly enough coffee.

EIGHT

The Man

"Thank you, Mrs. Zimmerman. He was a dream to work with. Do you want to schedule his next session now?" Amanda returned the woman's credit card, hoping not to be struck down by lightning for lying. Cookie was one of those dogs that actively disliked baths and spent most of the appointment trying to escape. Plus, he was a biter. Amanda had worn her thickest gloves and still had a couple of nips. He wasn't vicious. It was more of a game for Cookie. She didn't think he got a lot of walks.

"No, I'll call you. My widdle baby wooks so bweautiful. Look at him there." Mrs. Z patted the white-blonde curls on her head as she stood back and admired the miracle Amanda had performed on the *widdle baby*. "He could have been a show dog, you know? I just didn't want to put that pressure on him."

The Bichon Frise's double coat hadn't been tended to in a while, and Mrs. Z's preference for the distinctive cotton ball show cut left Cookie looking remarkably like his owner.

Amanda left while the happy owner and dog were making smoochy faces at each other and headed back to the Pink Pup.

Opening the door to the front cab, she called in, "You guys ready for lunch?"

Qbert thumped his tail.

Grok glared at her from the driver's seat. "Obviously, since you've left us starving for days. How is your hand?"

"He didn't even break the skin." Amanda smiled at Grok's gruff concern for her.

As soon as they had gotten to the Pink Pup, she'd convinced Grok to let her give him a bath. To her surprise, he had agreed, admitting he didn't want to stink all day. Before long, he'd been clean again and she'd been toweling him dry and checking him over for any injuries. She was still keeping an eye on the cat for any ill-effects from his morning spell, but as always, he had bounced back as if nothing had happened with no memory of the event.

She'd given him cat treats disguised in a beef jerky package so he wouldn't fuss about eating common cat food. It had satisfied him enough that she could get to her morning clients.

"Do you want Mexican or Greek for lunch? Or should we go to the Monarch Deli and get sandwiches and eat at the beach? Scoot over." Amanda motioned the cat out of her seat.

Grok turned and glared at Qbert. The dog's tail slowed its rhythmic beat, and he slid from the seat to the floorboard between the seats. Grok jumped into the passenger seat and took his place. "Aren't you forgetting that we're eating out tonight at the pub?"

"You're right. I forgot to call Dottie and tell her the plan changed. I'll do that at lunch. Mexican it is." Amanda got in and started the van.

All through her appointments, her mind had spun on the early morning events. "You know what I don't get—" She was interrupted by her phone ringing. Fishing the phone out of her pocket, she answered. "Pink Power Wash and Groom."

"Hi Amanda, it's Anh. I want to talk to you about your sister's sublease."

Amanda recognized the name as the neighbor who lived across the street. He and his wife had a travel agency in town. "What sublease?"

"Alexandra rented a portion of our agency's leased space as an office. She prepaid the rent for several months but not the electric bill, and it's a few days past due. We need to know what we should do." Anh spoke to someone else, the conversation muffled in the background, and then came back on the line. "I have a customer. Do you want to stop by and look at the office? You know where our travel agency is?"

Amanda hadn't known her sister had an office in town. Confused about what she had the right to do, she decided checking out the space seemed the best way to start. "Okay, I've got a free hour now. I'll meet you there in 20 minutes."

Anh agreed, and they hung up.

"We aren't going to get lunch either, are we?" Grok muttered from the passenger seat. His hind leg was sticking up in the air, and he was grooming the hair on the back of his thigh.

"We'll get lunch; it's just going to be a quick stop."

"Uh-huh," Grok hummed.

Qbert thumped his tail.

Driving through the town of Ocean Wood always made her smile. Cypress Avenue, the main street running through town, was lined on either side with shops and restaurants. The travel agency was a red brick building on the corner of Cypress and Grove Avenue, the town's primary cross streets. It was an excellent location.

Amanda pulled behind the red brick building and parked in the empty lot in the back. She knew her van would fit because she had seen Anh hide his RV there—the RV he had finally revealed to his wife he had purchased.

She slipped a lead on Qbert, and the cat and dog followed her to the front of the building. The doorbell jingled as they walked in. The travel agency was a decent-sized space sectioned into a customer lounge in the front, four tables with conference room-style seating, and stacks of brochures. The walls were lined with faded travel posters, and paper hearts hung from the ceiling, despite Valentine's Day being months ago. "Hello?"

There was a sound of something dropping in a back room, and Anh burst through the door. "Amanda! I didn't hear you come in. You found the place okay?" As he asked the question, he wiped his hands on his pants, clutching the fabric.

"No problem. Great parking. Is this a bad time?" Amanda added, seeing Anh was preoccupied.

"No, this is good. We're just cleaning—well, downsizing. We're going to sublet the desks in here to a tax company. They have a pop-up retail model, and we aren't getting a lot of walk-in traffic. It's a real win for us and will keep the agency going. But they need storage space, so we're sorting out the back. Come on. Let me show you your sister's office."

Amanda followed Anh out of the office to the street, where he opened the door next to his and motioned her to follow.

"Have you done any mushroom foraging lately?" Amanda asked.

Anh stopped and turned on her with a horrified expression. "What are you implying?"

Amanda's checks reddened. "I just meant you loved doing it and were part of a group, and sure, Vic was killed with a poison mushroom tart, but—"

"I haven't been able to look at a mushroom since that happened. I threw out all my old gear." Anh put his hand over his mouth, his face pale.

"I'm really sorry," Amanda whispered.

Shaking himself, Anh resumed walking, and she followed behind. They entered a small sitting area with an arched hallway and stairs leading up.

The man took a breath and recovered his business-like attitude. "Ownership of the property is up in the air right now. My wife, Amy, took over managing the building a few years ago. It got us a discount on our rent." Anh gave a brittle smile.

Amanda returned it with one that didn't reach her eyes.

"So, the agency has its own waiting room. All the other renters share this small lobby." He led them down a hall toward the back of the building. Anh stopped at the last door before the back exit, and Amanda waited for him to open it. She looked at him. He looked at her. "I don't have the key."

"Well, I don't have the key." Amanda grabbed the handle in frustration and shook it. The door swung open.

"That's strange. Alexandra always kept it locked." Anh stepped back.

Amanda started to step forward, but Grok pushed ahead, shoving the door open. The cat scanned the room. "It's been tossed. Alexandra wouldn't leave it like this," he declared.

Amanda made a sound of acknowledgment under her breath as she surveyed the office. It was rather bare, and the space had been ransacked. Files tossed, boxes and drawers dumped, furniture flipped.

"You should call the police." Anh hovered at the threshold.

As Amanda pushed into the room, Qbert's tail

drooped and he backed away, his feet slipping on the hard-wood floor.

Grok finished checking the room. "It's clear. Whoever did this is gone."

"Looks like whoever did it is long gone," Anh said, unable to understand Grok. His phone started ringing, "I've got to take this. Amy said if you wanted to pay the electric bill, you could use the space. She could probably cut you a key. The lease is paid up for the next three months, so why not? You can park your grooming van in the back and use this as a private waiting room for your dogs," Anh said quickly then waved a hand as he answered his phone.

"But—" Amanda started to say, but Anh was already gone.

"Did he really say I should work here?" she asked Grok.

"He did. It's a nice building. All the fire escapes are easy to climb, and they keep the access to the roof open. You can survey the whole town center from there. However, Alexandra didn't think it was secure and never kept anything important here." Grok batted at a pencil cup and sent it careening into a corner. "Evidently, she was correct."

"I can't take over the space. What would I do with it?" Sure, she had thought about getting an accessible retail space for clients who didn't want her driving to their homes. And it was right across the street from her primary source of referrals, the Best Friend Boutique. "I'm barely making enough money to keep gas in the van and feed you. Where would I get the money for rent?"

"Rent's paid for a while. Seems a shame to waste it." Grok clawed a cushion from a chair, circled it in both directions, and settled in.

"What do you think they were looking for?"

Grok surveyed the room. "Not much was important here, just old files. Alexandra used her laptop and her casebook for everything."

"Well, I've got her casebook locked up at home. But we never found her laptop. I thought she took it with her, but maybe whoever did this stole it."

Grok gave a bored yawn. "Maybe. Wake me when you've decided to stop starving us."

Amanda gaped at the cat.

Was he even going to help sort out this mess? And what craziness was he talking about—keep the place? She started to tidy up and then stopped. If she was going to report this, she shouldn't clean up. Wouldn't the police want to see what the space looked like after the break-in? She groaned. If she called the police, no matter if she called the main line or Detective Kim directly, the police chief was bound to find out and blame this on her.

Might as well get it over with. She pulled out her phone to call Detective Kim. When had she become the type of person who had the police on speed dial?

There was a sound at the door. A large man stood in the doorway. His big hand reached out a manicured finger at her. Gemstones glinted from the thick gold watch on his wrist as he shook his hand at her. "You lied to me, Alexandra."

NINE

Missing

"You know my sister?" Amanda felt her excitement rising. Maybe this man could help her find Alexandra. She moved towards him, stumbling over a stack of files on the floor and sending them sliding across the room.

"Don't play games with me. We had a deal, and you didn't hold up your end; I want it back." The bald man stepped forward, clenching his meaty hand into a fist and shaking it at her.

In a flash, Grok stood between them, the gray hair on his back raising as he hissed out a warning.

The man froze, eyes wide, his shiny head and animated expression making him less threatening. Then he smirked and took another step.

The sound of breaking glass from the front of the building caught their attention. Outside, footsteps rushed towards the sound.

The man shook his finger at Amanda again and ran off.

Amanda and Grok raced to the door. He was gone.

"Look, someone propped open the back door." Amanda pointed to where the door bounced against a brick.

"I can catch him," Grok said as tires squealed and a car roared out of the parking lot.

Amanda rushed to the door to catch his license plate, but only the smell of burning rubber lingered. When she turned back around, Grok was gone.

Returning to the office, Amanda picked up the phone she had dropped by the upside-down desk. She wondered about the state of the room. The overturned furniture had to be from the break-in, but the piles of files and the line of dirty coffee cups on the windowsill made her think that her sister kept a messy office. That gave her hope. Despite Grok saying Alexandra didn't keep anything important here, one of those files could hold the answer to her sister's disappearance.

The call to the detective was brief, and he promised to come right by.

Grok was panting as he padded back to the office. "By the time I got to the roof, he was gone. I don't know which direction he went."

"Did you recognize him?" Grok's mind was tricky. He knew nothing of his past, and even his short-term memory was affected by his sudden seizures. She didn't want to put him at risk, but anything he could recall might help them find her sister.

"Not him, but I recognized the scent. I only saw him from above, but I think he was the man following us this morning." Grok wrinkled up his nose and rubbed at it with his paw.

"His cologne was strong. He dressed like a mobster, and he threatened Alexandra. I think it's safe to say it was one of her clients or someone she was investigating. Do you think that is who broke in?"

Grok took a deep sniff. "No. I smell him just at the door. He wasn't our man."

A wave of disappointment washed over Amanda. That would have been too easy. "Well, I've called Detective Kim; he'll be here soon. Can you tell if anything was taken? If we can discover what they were looking for and if they found it, we might be able to learn more about Alexandra's disappearance."

Grok took a glance around the room. "Sure, but where's the dog?"

"What?" Amanda spun in a circle—no Qbert. Rushing to a window, she scanned the back parking lot— no Qbert. She raced past Grok and down the hall to the travel agency. They hadn't seen the dog.

She had lost Qbert.

Amanda and Grok walked several blocks around the building looking for Qbert. Grok picked up the dog's scent in the town center but lost it by the dumpster behind the Lighthouse Pub.

Amanda glanced at the time on her phone. "I need to go back to the office and meet Detective Kim."

Grok's nose surfed the ground, his nostrils flaring as he took in sniffs of air. "I'll keep trying to pick up the scent again."

On her way back, Amanda called the neighbors, Dot and Frank, asking them to be on the lookout at her sister's house, since Qbert was familiar with the area and might have headed home. She also told them about the change in their dinner plans, with Ben unable to celebrate on his new boat. She just hoped he was still talking to her by then.

When she entered the office, the detective stood by the desk surveying the room. "Do you always keep the door unlocked?"

"It's my first time here. I didn't know Alexandra had an office." She righted a chair and dropped her purse onto it.

The detective made a note in his book. "Any idea when this happened?"

"No. And, honestly, I can't tell what's clutter and what's ransacked. I had no idea Alexandra was this messy. I just thought you should see it before I started cleaning up."

The detective pulled out a camera and snapped a few photos. "I hate to tell you, but this doesn't look recent. And with the door unlocked, anyone could have had access. I'll file a report in case Alexandra needs it to make a claim with her insurance company, but we don't have the staff to investigate right now."

A warmth flooded Amanda's body as the detective

assumed her sister's return. Sometimes, it felt like she was the only one who cared that her sister was missing. "Why aren't the police trying to find her? I filed a missing person report, but nothing happened."

"People are looking into her disappearance, but it's not unusual for her to be gone weeks or longer on a case. Not much can be done unless we find signs of foul play."

Amanda threw her hands up in the air. "Foul play? Like a body being found in her house? Her cat being left without care? Her office being broken into?"

Detective Kim lowered the camera. "We know why the body was there, and you helped prove it had nothing to do with your sister's disappearance. Care for Grok was arranged with a neighbor. And we don't know when this break-in occurred or what they took. It could have been one of her cases." His voice softened. "I know you're worried. But believe me, people who have known her for a long time are following up. I can't tell you more than that."

Amanda wondered if he meant Chief of Police Gina Rodriguez or if someone else was on the case. She wished she knew what was going on. She had found her sister's casebook when she first arrived. Written in code, neither Ben nor Amanda had been able to break it. Maybe it was time she worked harder to find out what that book said.

"I've got everything I need for my report. I'll stop and talk to Anh and Amy on my way out. You can clean up or whatever you want to do with the office. You said Alexandra already paid the sublease rent. Are you thinking about using the space?"

"I'm not sure yet. It still feels very invasive to me."

"I think your sister would want you to make yourself at home." The detective gave a quick nod and left.

Amanda wished she could be as confident in her sister's welcome.

TEN

The Library

Amanda pushed out her afternoon appointments to keep searching for Qbert. She caught up with Grok on the grounds of the post office. "Have you seen him?"

The cat stopped to double check a scent. "He came this direction."

"I'll ask in the post office if anyone saw him." Amanda returned a few minutes later with no news.

They carried on, Grok sniffing and Amanda stopping in every shop and restaurant they passed.

It was almost an hour later when she got the call.

Jill Anne Meyers was a local mushroom forager and head librarian at the Ocean Wood Public Library.

"Amanda, I've been trying to reach Ben, but he isn't answering his phone. Do you know where I can find him? We've got something of a problem in the reading room."

Amanda waved a hand at Grok to get his attention. "He might have his phone off. Is this about Qbert?"

"You could say that." The head librarian's tone was the one she used to wrangle dozens of rowdy children to silence.

The library was two blocks from where they were searching and just off the main street. It only took a couple of minutes to jog there. The stucco building with tall arched windows and a tile roof took up the whole block. The library faced a park with a small grove of tall redwood trees. A pair of Monarch butterflies weaved around a white gazebo.

When they arrived, Ms. Meyers gave them a stern look as she held the door open. She quickly led them past the staff desk through the book stacks and reading room and through another set of doors to a glassed-in meeting room. The children's brightly lit reading area was in the corner of this space, and it looked like an event was happening. Dozens of small children clustered around a colorful carpet with a giant bean bag.

Ms. Meyers pointed in the direction of the event. Her lips twitched, and the stern look dissolved into a big smile. "He's been very popular with our young patrons, but perhaps it's time he went home."

A small girl, four or five years old, spotted them as they approached the group. One pigtail had freed itself, and she was wearing a miniature neon fireman's jacket with a rainbow tutu, butterfly wings, and a manic expression. She pulled her thumb out of her mouth with a pop and pointed a wet finger at Grok. "Look! Big kitty!"

Grok froze. He started to back away as if a bear had

spotted him. But it was too late. A group of toddlers attacked. They tugged at his fur, swung his tail like a jump rope, and several declared he was big enough to ride like a pony.

As the group magnetized to Grok, Amanda saw what had been holding their attention. Qbert was lying on the bean bag in the center of the reading area. At least six children were using him as a pillow, and dozens of colorful elastic bands and barrettes styled his fur.

When Amanda approached him to put on the lead, Qbert had a blissed-out look from the attention. She snapped the lead on his collar and tugged on the leash. Several children cried out in dismay, and one burst into tears.

"Sorry, but Qbert has to go home now." Amanda backed towards the door, unsure if turning her back on the emotional mini humans was safe. She groaned when she realized she was starting to sound like the grumpy cat. That reminded her, and she called out, "Come on, Grok."

He exploded from the surrounding group, almost levitating in his haste to escape.

Ms. Meyers walked them out. "Thank you for coming, but maybe it would be best if you don't return and ask Ben to keep Qbert away. This visit has been too stimulating for the younger patrons."

Amanda agreed and promised she would be alone if she returned.

"I heard about poor Tobias. Do they know how it happened?" Ms. Meyers asked.

Amanda did a double take at the woman's comment. "The police released information?"

"It's not general knowledge, no. My nephew Andrew works for the Medical Examiner's office. He was in line for the job before Ben came along." She sniffed.

"Maybe I should be asking you what the police know. Did Andrew say anything about what they had found?"

"That's right... Ben was removed from the case. Shame. But my family aren't gossips. The police will tell us what has happened when they're good and ready. Of course, everyone knows you found another body. Couldn't keep that a secret in a small town."

Amanda's eyebrows drew together, and she resisted the urge to look around. Was everyone in the library looking at her? "I didn't know news traveled that fast, but Detective Kim is on the case. I'm sure he will do a good job."

"I expect he will. He was always a studious young man, not like Tobias. We should have expected that boy's luck to run out one day." The woman held open the outside door for them.

"What do you mean?" Amanda paused on the threshold, resisting Qbert's tugging on the leash.

"Tobias had so much potential. He was an early reader. But he got bored easily and liked a challenge. He was a bit of a finder. If you needed something hard to locate, he could usually find it for you. He even found me a lost edition of *Myths and Shadows: Paranormal Encounters in the Santa Cruz Mountains*. Your sister recommended it. Oh, and he always had something to sell, not always legally.

He had been running on luck for years, barely staying off the police radar. I imagine it was just a matter of time before his luck ran out." The woman clucked her tongue and, with a nod at the outside, ushered Amanda out of the library. The door slid shut behind them.

ELEVEN

The Call

Amanda had pushed all her appointments back to look for Qbert. Now, she was rushing to make up the time. She jogged up the sidewalk to her client's Craftsman-style home and knocked.

"Hello, Mr. Martin." Amanda waved at the man in the business suit and wild curly hair who opened the door.

"Hi, Amanda. Coco is ready for you."

They exchanged pleasantries, and she accepted the Standard Poodle's leash.

On the way back to the van, her phone rang.

"Is this the woman from the pink-something dog grooming service?" the caller asked.

"Yes, I run the Pink Power Wash and Groom. Can I help you?" Amanda tucked the phone between her ear and shoulder and fumbled with the RV door, finally getting it open and leading Coco inside.

"I saw your van this morning at the marina. My two

puppies need a spa day. Can you be here in fifteen minutes?" the woman asked.

"I'm fully booked this afternoon. I can try to fit you in tomorrow."

"That's inconvenient for us. I'll find someone better." The woman hung up.

Amanda stared at the phone in disbelief. She never turned down work. But she couldn't cancel her other client. Amanda was still miffed as she started Coco's bath in the back of the Pink Pup. Why would anyone make a demand like that without any account for someone else's schedule? Wait a minute—could that have been the woman from the marina with the twin Pekingese, Poppy and Daisy? Amanda squinted in thought. What was that woman's name? Erkle? Sterling? Erling? That was it. Luna Erling. Amanda was itching to get her hands on her dogs' coats. She shouldn't have turned the work down. She was fully booked, but she could have tried harder to negotiate a different time.

Amanda stewed about the missed opportunity as she rushed through the rest of her day.

She was late to meet Ben and the others for dinner and drove directly to the Lighthouse Pub.

After a quick cleanup in the RV bathroom, where she splashed water on her face, and switched her T-shirt and jeans with the spare she kept for work emergencies, which happened almost daily, she declared herself "as good as it gets" and headed inside.

They were the last to arrive when she walked in with Grok and Qbert. The Lighthouse Pub wasn't fancy enough to attract many tourists, so the locals used it as a meetup place. It had a beer garden and patio seating, but it was way too cold in the evenings to sit outside, even with the heat lamps blasting hot air. The interior was painted a warm mocha and felt cozy. People stood at the bar or moved between wooden tables to greet each other.

Amanda searched the crowd for her group. She finally spotted Albert's electric wheelchair in a corner and headed that direction.

Her entourage got a few strange looks, but Amanda pushed on, hoping they wouldn't be kicked out because of the animals.

The minute Qbert saw Ben, he lunged. Leaping up, he tried to fit on Ben's lap but resigned himself to just putting his paws on his chest and getting in his face, telling him with excited yaps about his day. Amanda had left his stylized hair in place, and Ben examined the effect of a dozen bands and barrettes on his sheepdog's coat.

"We wondered if you would be joining us today. Hope you didn't lose anything on the way here." Dot chuckled at her joke. Dot was the first person she'd talked to when she arrived in Ocean Wood. The octogenarian with the adrenaline addiction and her husband Albert were back-yard neighbors and had befriended her immediately.

"How did you find out he escaped?" Amanda sank into a seat.

Albert patted the back of her hand. "How do you think? I live at the hub of the gossip grapevine. Now tell us what really happened."

Amanda told them about her day's adventures, including the strange man who visited her sister's tossed office.

"We knew about Tobias. Sad, such a young man. And everyone has heard about Qbert's adventure at the library. But this guy from the office, you don't know who he was?" Frank leaned forward, folding his beefy arms on the table and studying Amanda with a frown.

Frank lived across the street and was the second person she had met when she arrived. A former city council member and recovering workaholic, he knew everyone in town.

"No. Does he sound familiar to any of you?" Amanda asked the group.

"A bald, mafioso-looking man in a suit with an expensive watch? That would stand out around here." Dot waved her arm around the room. "Well, the suit would, wouldn't it, Bertie? None of the squares around here wear anything fancier than a polo shirt!" Dot slapped her husband's arm and bent over laughing.

"I know most of the suit-wearers in this town, mostly politicians or real estate agents, and he doesn't sound familiar. Maybe he's from the Bay Area or SoCal." Frank leaned back and patted his protruding belly. "Let's order. Dinner is on me tonight. We might not be celebrating

Ben's new home, but we can still celebrate being together."

Dottie let out a cheer, and Albert gave the larger man a few friendly claps on the shoulder in agreement.

As the others perused the menu, Amanda took the opportunity to apologize to Ben for losing Qbert. Ben had wrapped his arms around his dog and wasn't even letting go to look at the menu. "Are you okay?" Amanda asked.

"It's been a hard day." Ben rubbed his nose into Qbert's hair, bumping into one of the barrettes.

Ben couldn't do his job, his boat was half underwater, and Amanda had played a prime role in nearly losing his dog—of course he was having a bad day.

"I thought I might find you here," said a voice from the door.

Ben and Amanda looked up. Gina Rodriguez had entered the pub with her husband, Mario. Even in casual clothes, the woman commanded the room's attention, and the murmur in the pub died down.

"What's this I hear about a break-in at Alexandra's office? How did you manage that in your busy day?" She gave Amanda a stern glare.

"I didn't do the breaking in," Amanda protested.

"You need to stay away from Alexandra's office and her cases. You may be staying in her house, but *you* are not *her*. She is an experienced investigator, and has worked for dangerous people. You could get yourself, and her, into a lot of trouble poking your nose where it doesn't belong."

"Have you heard from her? Is she working on a case?" Amanda leaned forward, clenching her hands together.

"I didn't say that. Just when she returns, she isn't going to appreciate her cases being messed with."

"I imagine she will appreciate her office being tossed even less. I have no intention of invading my sister's personal space, but obviously someone else did, and maybe if you were actively investigating her disappearance—"

"Feel free to stop by the office and follow up on the missing-person case you filed. I'll make sure to tell the investigator to start by re-examining your sudden appearance in town."

The chief then turned away from Amanda to Ben.

Ben paled.

"We got the time of death, just before midnight. As you have no alibi for that time—"

"I'm a suspect," Ben concluded for her.

The woman pursed her lips. "I didn't say that. We just need more information before you can be cleared to work the case. You'll be hearing from your supervisor." With disapproving looks to the animals, she turned and stalked off, her husband trailing behind her.

Ben accepted the sympathy and pats of solidarity from the table. But after a couple of minutes, he closed his menu.

At Amanda's questioning look, he admitted, "Not hungry, and I'm really tired. Besides, Qbert isn't supposed to be inside. I think we'll head home. Well, back to the boat."

Frank leaned forward again. "Isn't it leaking?"

"We've drained most of the water, and there's a temporary patch over the leak. I want to keep an eye on it tonight and make sure it sticks."

"Stay." Dot grabbed at Ben's hand. "Let us cheer you up."

He squeezed her fingers then released her hand and said his goodbyes. As Ben left, Qbert trailed behind on his leash, scooping up discarded fries he found along the way.

Ben was the best person Amanda knew. He gave so much to his job and had built Ocean Wood's new medical examiner's department from scratch. Would he be fired over this? Amanda couldn't help but feel that she had somehow let Ben down. Why could she never take care of the people that depended on her?

"Well, we can do nothing for him, so this had better not interrupt our dinner." Grok jumped up on Ben's vacant chair, ignoring the shocked look from the table beside them. "After missing breakfast and lunch, I've got my eye on the salmon, but those crab cakes look good too, especially if Frank is buying."

Amanda glanced around at the patrons staring at them. She would give the cat a piece of her mind later. Now, she couldn't stop thinking about the murder. Ben had done so much for her since she arrived in town. She couldn't just watch him get pushed around this way with no one standing up for him. It was so unfair. There had to be something she could do to find out what happened at the marina. She didn't want to let down another person she cared about.

She turned to the rest of the table. "Hey, you guys want to help me try to solve a murder?"

TWELVE

Dreamy

D ottie leaned in. "Heck yeah!"

Albert grabbed her glass of wine to keep it from flying.

"What did you have in mind? I'm not much for take-downs, but I did keep ornery Dave Naff from filibustering a council meeting once, so I'm not afraid of a challenge."

Albert turned his chair to look at Frank. "Was that the Dave who runs the mushroom farm in the Santa Cruz hills?"

"No, that's the other Dave."

"The bee farmer from the valley?"

"No, that's the other, other, Dave. This is the developer."

"Ah, he was a skunk."

Dot nodded in support of her husband's claim. Then she turned to Amanda "What do you want us to do?"

"I figure we don't have to actually find the killer. We just have to discover enough to clear Ben's name.

"Okay, so what do you know so far?" Albert asked.

Amanda told them what she had learned from the librarian about Tobias's skill set.

Dottie nodded. "She isn't kidding. The guy was a wiz at being in the right place at the right time. He once walked by an ATM, and it just started spitting out cash at him."

Albert shook his head. "That was after he had already broken into the machine."

Amanda directed them back. "The chief says the time of death was just before midnight. But I'm not sure what to do next."

Grok gave her a strange look then seemed to shake his head and went back to grooming.

"Oooh. I know what you have to do. I saw this on *Castle*. That guy is so hot—" Dot's face got a dreamy look.

Albert coughed. "Focus."

"Right, so on the show, it's all about the usual motive, means, and opportunity. Meaning, you have to figure out who had access to the marina at the time the diver was killed."

"Well, that would be everyone with a boat, right?" Amanda groaned. There were a lot of boats there.

"Sure, but most of them just store their boat there. The police will probably pull the records with the information who keyed in. And then, someone could have snuck in, or swum in, or boated in and out." Frank listed a few other ways people could get access.

Amanda's resolve to help Ben started to falter.

"That is too much. She will never be able to do all that.

She needs to start small," Albert spoke up with the voice of reason. "Start with who do you *know* was there? Who did you see that morning?"

"Close enough to see something? Well, that would be the Erlings and crew in the boat next to Ben. Also, Robin the sailing instructor and Jack Roberts—he manages the marina."

"Oh, I know Jack. Never liked him. He's a good one to start with. I'd love to know what he's hiding." Frank rubbed his hands together.

"She isn't looking for dirt for you. She's looking for motive and a weapon. As Castle would say in his growly voice"—Dottie affected a deep voice— "we need to know who had a reason and means to kill Tobias."

Amanda laughed and felt some of the tension she had been carrying around ease. She didn't know exactly how she would do it, but she was going to try to do something to help Ben. "Hey Dottie, do David Tennant's voice."

THIRTEEN

Found 'Em

Something didn't sit right in Grok's belly. And it wasn't the thought of choosing between salmon and crab. Maybe it was this murder Amanda had embroiled herself in. She was a trouble magnet, the same as her sister. Amanda's friend Ben was at the heart of it this time. He was a nice guy in a soft, squishy way, but he had interrupted two meals today and almost a third, which would take some time to forgive.

The server returned to their table with their drinks, freezing when he placed Ben's beer in front of Grok. "Uh, I don't think cats are allowed inside."

Another waiter stopped him. "It's okay. He's a service animal."

"He is?" Their server ran a skeptical eye over the cat.

A growl rumbled up Grok's throat.

"Yeah, she worked it out with the owners of several restaurants in town after the cat helped catch those vandals last summer, the ones who did all the property damage and almost burned down the historic Roja Adobe. He's in here all the time." She dipped her head to Amanda.

"I did? I did!" Amanda nodded so hard her hair slapped her face.

The servers moved on.

Grok stifled a laugh. Amanda was a terrible liar. He had a fuzzy recollection of a fire and Alexandra cutting a deal, sorting it out, and taking care of things as she always did. He knew he didn't often express it, but he missed her and wished he could remember why she left. He couldn't figure out why everyone confused the twins; they smelled utterly different. Amanda was fruity shampoo and a hundred dog breeds, and Alexandra had been... He searched his memory and plucked steel and leather out before a needle of agony pierced his head. Why could he recall some things clearly, while others were behind a foggy veil of pain? He backed off from trying to remember more.

Grok shifted in his seat and took a minute to groom his paw. It was disgusting how humans ate with their hands and didn't even clean them first. While he licked between his toes, he contemplated his earlier unease.

It was the two people with hoods over their heads who watched the male, Ben, while he was here that had triggered his alarm. They were too far away to get a clear scent on in the crowded room. But their behavior was suspicious, and soon after Ben left, they had a quick whisper fight and followed. What were they up to? Were they after Ben and Qbert? Was one of them the killer? Grok didn't like the idea of a murderer wandering around his town.

He gave a last lick then slipped off the chair. Grok

crossed the room, weaving in and out of people's legs. Filtering through the smells coming from the kitchen and wafting off each of the bodies around him, he started to catch the scent of his prey. He followed the path of the hooded humans as they trailed Ben out the back exit.

When he got there the back door was closed. Grok growled at the obstacle. From beyond the foggy veil in his mind, an old image surfaced of staring at doors until they opened. He quickly let the memory go, as he didn't want to be derailed from his mission by a headache or worse. But what could it hurt to try?

He focused his attention on the door, the handle, and visualized it turning.

Nothing happened.

He kept staring at the handle until the headache returned and he started to feel groggy.

A noise sounded behind Grok. Turning his head, he watched a woman leave the kitchen. She hung her apron on a hook then grabbed a bag and headed out the back door.

Grok slipped out behind her.

So much time had passed that he was not surprised that Ben was nowhere in sight. But the two hooded people he followed were arguing farther down the alley. Maybe they hadn't been after the doctor.

Grok turned to go back inside, but the door slammed closed. Frustration rumbled in his throat.

An angry shout echoed through the dark alley as the argument increased in volume.

"Obviously it wouldn't be a problem if you had done your job." The taller figure loomed over the shorter one.

Their hoods hid their identity, but not their scent. The larger one smelled like nut butter, citrus, and something familiar. Where had he experienced that scent before? It was a man, Grok was sure, and his voice held the tone of maturity. The shorter one's voice was hard to place as male or female, and they smelled like the ocean, coconut, and beer.

"I *was* doing my job, but you interfered. Now what do we do?" Coconut Beer moved restlessly but didn't push the taller one away.

Nut Butter's tone was dark as he loomed over the shorter figure. "You find them—"

Grok's ears perked up, but he still missed the rest of the comment.

"He wasn't supposed to have them." Nut Butter must have anticipated an attempt to escape; they wrapped a fist in Coconut Beer's jacket and slammed them back into the brick wall.

Grok had been keeping his distance, which he now realized was ridiculous; he was a cat. They would not find his presence in an alley suspicious. He wanted to see their faces.

A door banged behind him.

Grok shot straight into the air and landed on the top of the dumpster. He turned and snarled the direction of the noise.

The man at the door screamed. He clutched a bag of

what smelled like trash to his chest. "You scared me half to death, big kitty."

"Call me that again, and I'll take care of the other half," Grok growled, knowing the young man wouldn't understand him but feeling compelled to make the offer anyway. Grok turned back to the two figures he had been watching.

They were gone.

Jumping off the dumpster, Grok hurried over to sniff the space where they had been. He smelled human urine on the wall, rotten produce on the ground, and the lingering scent of the humans, but nothing he could use.

A growl rumbled deep in Grok's throat. The people were gone, and now another meal had been disrupted by stupid human stuff. He followed the trash guy back into the pub, hoping to redeem his dinner.

"Where have you been? I didn't even see you leave," Amanda whispered from the side of her mouth when Grok returned to their table, jumping up on the chair next to her.

The menus were gone, and everyone was deep into their drinks. At the other end of the table, Dot clutched at Albert and laughed hysterically at a joke.

"Did I miss ordering?" Grok hissed out his displeasure, knowing he had.

Amanda covered her mouth with her hand as she responded to his question. "You did, but I got something for you. The crab cakes were on sale, so I got a double order. We can share."

Grok purred. There were times when he thought

Amanda wasn't that bad. Then he remembered he had news for her.

Amanda listened wide-eyed as he told her what he'd heard in the alley.

"Who do you think they were?" Amanda pretended to look in her purse as she asked Grok the question out of the side of her mouth.

"I don't know. But I've got their scent now, so I might recognize them the next time I smell them." Grok turned in his chair. Once, twice, three times till he got it just right and settled to wait for his meal.

Amanda tapped her lips with a finger, a far-off look in her eyes. "We need to return to the marina."

Frank turned towards Amanda. "Did you say something?"

Amanda shook her head, her hair smacking her face again, and Grok resisted the urge to chase it. She stuttered out an excuse. "I was worrying about a job I gave up today. Someone wanted me to drop everything and come right over to them. I don't like saying no to people."

Frank leaned towards them to be heard over the loud noise from the bar. "Can't say I missed that side of the business. Being in real estate was an adrenaline rush, but my pottery studio is enough for me now." Grok smelled the insincerity behind Frank's words.

Their food soon arrived, and Amanda tried to put Grok's plate on the chair next to him, but there wasn't room. She finally gave up and left it on the table. Grok couldn't care less about the strange looks he received as he dug in. The pub was warm, he didn't sense any threats, and he had a plate of fish. Life was good.

FOURTEEN

Bunnies

Amanda woke with a start, her heart pounding erratically against her ribcage. The night had been a relentless onslaught of bad dreams, each more harrowing than the last, to the final one where she was endlessly fleeing through a shadowy maze, chased by her past failures that took on the shape of fuzzy pink human-sized bunnies. She shivered.

A quick glance out the window showed the fog drifting through the backyard and blotting out the backyard neighbors' homes. It reminded her how alone she was.

A loud snore sounded behind her.

Well, not completely alone.

Grok slept in the center of the bed, spread wide and drooling on the bedspread.

Amanda let him be and shivered again as she stuffed her feet into slippers, grabbing the heavy sweater she kept at the foot of the bed as she shuffled off to the kitchen to make coffee.

It was mornings like this where she got all up in her head, doubting herself and second guessing every decision she had made in life. But she didn't regret leaving Ohio or searching out her sister. This fresh start was scary, but it felt right. She just needed to anchor herself in the present and shake off the cobwebs.

She paced the kitchen while waiting for the coffee to brew, her thoughts whirling. Amanda didn't know if it was her indecisiveness over declining the "spa day" job or her worry about Ben that had trigger bad dreams, but she knew she had to do something. Pulling her phone from the sweater pocket, she dialed Ben's number.

No answer.

She tried again. Same result.

"I should go check on him." Once the thought had occurred to her, she had trouble letting it go. Sure, she could stop by and see him later today, but he had looked so miserable last night, and some instinct was driving her to hunt him down now.

Amanda hurried into the bedroom and shook the still-sleeping cat. "We need to find Ben and talk to him." After pulling off pajamas, she pulled on a pair of jeans.

Grok blinked open his eyes and glared at her through the arms of the pajamas that had landed on his head. "Why? Is he lost?"

"I don't know. I just—I need to find Ben," she told the cat, not able to justify the instinct in the moment. Then muttered for her own benefit, "I want to make sure he's okay."

Grok sat up. He swayed a little and stared around him as if trying to decide if he was being punked.

Amanda grabbed her coat and keys. "You coming?"

By the time she turned off the coffee pot, locked the front door, and started the RV, Grok had found his way to the passenger seat, though he didn't look any more awake.

Driving along the coast at this early hour, it only took a few minutes to cross town and arrive at the marina where the fog was starting to lift. Amanda was pulling the RV into the parking lot when she spotted Ben's car. Something moved in the window. It was a sock-covered foot pressed against the glass. She pulled up alongside the vehicle and parked.

"He doesn't look like he was expecting you," Grok commented.

"Why is he sleeping in his car?" Amanda popped out of the driver's seat and crossed to the other side of the RV. She bent over to look into the car's window. Ben was in the driver's seat, half reclined and curled uncomfortably around a pillow.

There was a snuffling sound from behind him, and Amanda squinted to see Qbert stretched out along the back seat, passed out.

"Ben?" Amanda knocked on the glass.

"I'll move the car, officer. Just give me a minute." Ben rolled his face deeper into the pillow to block a stray ray of morning light that had broken through the fog.

"Ben? Did you sleep here?" Amanda could tell the answer, but she still asked.

Waking with a sharp inhale, Ben blinked his eyes open. "Where am I?"

"In the marina parking lot." Amanda leaned her arms against the window frame as she watched him sit up and look around.

Ben saw her and started the engine long enough to roll down the window. Then he turned it off and, with a groan, slid back and closed his eyes. "What do you want, Amanda?"

"Why didn't you come to Alexandra's house? You could have stayed with us." Amanda's shoulders drooped.

Ben covered his eyes with his arm, and a flush swept up his neck. "I was embarrassed. I bought a boat. A leaky boat. I can't sleep on the boat because it's a crime scene, and I can't work because they think I might be a suspect."

Amanda didn't know what to say, and the silence stretched between them.

Then Ben sighed. "Ever since I lost my wife, I've been trying to say *yes* to new things. New town, new job, new friends, new place. But right now, I just want to go back to San Francisco to the way everything was before."

Leave town? Amanda pinched her lips together. She had been right. Ben really did need a friend this morning. She put a hand through the window and squeezed his arm. "Why don't we go back to the house and we can talk. I can cancel my morning appointments and make you breakfast."

"Appointments?" Ben sat up. "What time is it?"

Amanda told him the time, and Ben jerked his seat upright and turned the keys in the ignition. "I'm late! I'm meeting this morning with my department head, the mayor, the chief... Everyone will be there but me."

The engine turned over, and Amanda jumped back from the car.

"Sorry, Amanda. I have to go." Ben sped off.

Feeling stunned and more than a little disappointed, Amanda automatically answered her phone when it rang.

"Hello? Is this Amanda?" the voice on the other end asked when she didn't say anything.

"Oh, yes, sorry, this is Amanda, Pink Power...and all that."

"Hello, this is Tina Hanes, sorry, dear, but I have to cancel this morning. Next week, alright? Bye deary."

"What just happened?" Grok had found his way out of the RV.

Amanda shook her head, bewildered. Then she straightened her spine. "You know what? That's what I'm going to find out."

FIFTEEN

Schedule Change

A quick scroll through yesterday's calls, and she hit redial. It rang and rang before a groggy woman's voice answered. "Hello?"

"Good morning, Mrs. Erling. This is Amanda Warren from Pink Power Wash and Groom. We met recently…" Amanda trailed off, unsure if the name would jog any memories so early in the morning.

"Umm…" There was a pause, the sound of rustling sheets, and a quiet yawn. "Yes, good hair, bad nails. I remember." The voice was thick with sleep, barely coherent.

"We talked about a spa day for your Pekingese. I was wondering if you'd still like to go ahead with that today?" Amanda pushed on, hoping to seize the opportunity. "I'm available this morning if that works for you."

"Oh," The voice was heavy.

Had she gone back to sleep?

"Mrs. Erling?"

"Yes, the girls love spa days... Did we schedule something?"

Amanda pushed as much enthusiasm in her voice as she could, aiming for bright and hopeful. "Not exactly, but I'm free now and thought it might be a good time."

"K." There was a brief silence then a soft snore.

Amanda wasn't sure what to do, so she ended the call and exhaled a breath she hadn't realized she'd been holding. Well, that went better than expected.

"Are you coming?" she asked Grok, hoping for his support as she recovered her morning schedule and kicked off her own investigation.

"Are you kidding?" He raised a brow and cocked his head. "I'm going to find breakfast."

As Grok padded off, Amanda headed for the fence that separated the docks of the marina from the rest of the town. Near the gate, she spotted the skipper, Jeffrey Cook, whom she had met yesterday, having an intense exchange with a woman. He waved a greeting but continued his conversation. She recognized the sailing instructor, Robin McArthur.

As Amanda hurried towards them, the other woman left without a backward glance, heading towards a car parked on the far side of the lot, closer to the clubhouse.

"Hello!" Amanda called to the skipper, pasting on a smile. Her neighbors had gotten distracted last night and not been very helpful in coming up with a plan but after her night of bad dreams and Ben's comment on leaving, she was more determined than ever to follow through on the investigation.

Like a light switch had been flipped, the skipper's scowl turned to a smile. He responded in a robust voice. "Beautiful day, isn't it?"

Amanda scanned the marina. The final remnants of the morning fog had been hiding a vivid blue sky that contrasted sharply with the white boats bobbing in a gentle breeze. Seagulls glided above, calling to each other, and nearby sea lions barked. The light wind freshened the air with the taste of salt.

"It is." Amanda held out her hand to shake.

The skipper accepted, gripping her hand in his two big ones and staring intently into her eyes. "How are you today? Have you recovered from the shock of yesterday morning?"

"It was a surprise to find a body," Amanda admitted, clearing her throat.

The skipper squeezed her hand then released it and turned towards the marina entrance. "Are you headed this way?"

"Yes, I'm actually going to your boat. It's doggy spa day."

"Ah, of course." He quickly tapped in a gate code and held the door open for her when the gate unlocked.

"I didn't see you yesterday morning once the police arrived. Did you leave again?"

The skipper smiled. "I'm a working captain. There is very little downtime. If we aren't going somewhere, arriving from somewhere, or packing for somewhere, then there is never ending maintenance on a yacht."

Amanda had to admit that made sense. Still, she had to wonder. "So the police didn't question you?"

"Oh, they did."

They were walking side-by-side, and Amanda wished she could study his face. With her furry clients, she could tell by how they avoided her eyes if they had been up to something. Maybe it was the same with humans as it was with dogs.

"Have the police learned anything new?" Amanda cringed as she blundered out the question. Smooth. She wasn't off to a good start with her investigation.

"I wouldn't know. I'm not connected to the authorities here. What have you heard?"

Amanda hesitated. It wasn't confidential information if the police were telling her. It couldn't hurt to tell the skipper and find out if he had an alibi. "They say the time of death was just before midnight. Were you at the marina then? Did you see anything?"

The skipper paused then shook his head and kept walking. "Midnight? No, I wasn't here; I was at the Elysian Wave Lodge with the others. Maybe one of the liveaboards saw something?"

"Do you always stay in a hotel when you visit?" Amanda asked.

"We usually stay on the boat, but the Erlings have several events in town and opted to stay at the lodge this time. Most boats you see here are parked and the owners only come when they're taking them out."

"This might be a strange question, but is it normal for people to have spearguns on board?" Amanda had never seen one before and wasn't sure what they looked like.

"No. That's a separate sport from yachting. The marina keeps basic yachting equipment for its members but not usually hunting gear. You should ask Jack; he was a big hunter back in the day. His diver, Tobias, might have been into it. Maybe that was what they were yelling about when we arrived." As the skipper spoke, his long legs were quickly carrying him across the docks, and Amanda hurried to keep up.

"Jack and Tobias were fighting the day before he died?"

They arrived at the sizeable luxurious vessel parked next to Ben's. "Sounded like it. Here we are."

"It's a beautiful yacht," Amanda said, admiring the cruiser.

"It's a cramped boat." A look of distaste flickered across the skipper's face, quickly replaced by a crooked smile and a shrug. He held out a hand and helped Amanda step onto the back. "I prefer the larger one we have in San Diego. But this is a nice commuter for shorter trips."

"What do you mean, cramped?" Amanda stared up at the massive boat.

"It's just 65 feet and only sleeps eight, so the crew quarters are crammed here in the back of the bathing platform." Jeffrey pointed to a small hatch that didn't look large enough for Grok to slip through, let alone a grown man.

They climbed the first set of steps and had just reached the next level when hairballs of fury targeted the skipper.

The little dogs skidded across the deck and latched onto the skipper's pant legs like he was an invading pirate.

Jeffrey cursed and glanced around before shaking his leg.

"Hey, that's enough," Amanda spoke in a strong voice to the dogs. She expected the same treatment and braced herself, but they were surprised to see her and immediately released the skipper to race back into the yacht's main cabin, their little claws clicking across the wooden deck.

Amanda was stunned by the attack. What would have caused them to react that way?

"What are you doing here?" asked a sleepy voice from inside the main cabin. Curved sliding doors opened as the pair of dogs excitedly raced out again, greeted Amanda, paused to bark at the skipper, then bolted back into the cabin.

"You're on your own." Jeffrey raised his hands in mock surrender and walked away.

SIXTEEN

Spa Day

The inside of the yacht was sleek and modern, dominated by a cream color scheme and accented with teak wood and smoky glass. A large, curved seating area took up the center of the room. Luna Erling was reclining on the sofa, high-heeled slipper bobbing on one toe and a silk robe falling off a tan shoulder. She ignored Amanda and raised a hand to her mouth and yawned. "Mateo, is my breakfast ready yet?"

She directed her question towards the galley, where a muscular man in a white uniform had just turned off a blender. "Yes, ma'am." He uncapped the container and then poured the frothy purple mixture into a glass. He used a white ceramic knife to slice into a whole strawberry and added it to the edge of the glass. Inserting a stainless-steel straw, he carried the glass over to Mrs. Erling.

The woman accepted the drink with a flirty smile. "What about my babies? They're hungry, too." She pouted.

"I thought they might prefer to eat after their treatment. We don't want their little tummies getting upset." The man gave her a slow smile then retreated to the kitchen area.

"That is a good idea. You never know how dogs are going to respond to grooming," Amanda injected, not sure if she should introduce herself. She swayed as she shifted her weight from one foot to the other.

"Oh, that's right. That is why you're here." The woman put the untouched drink on the glass coffee table and turned to the two sable-colored Pekinese spooned into her side. "Would my little darlings like a massage?"

The dogs lapped up the attention.

"You do provide massages, right?" The woman arched a perfectly sculpted brow at her.

"Oh, yes. I suggest a 10-minute mud massage to help their coats shine. It really relaxes dogs before their bath. There is also a fizzy paw bath bomb I can use during their baths."

"Excellent. Those both sound perfect." Mrs. Erling picked up her drink again.

"Yesterday's incident must have been stressful for them—difficult for all of you, really." Amanda studied Mrs. Erling for a reaction. She couldn't think of any reason that the sophisticated woman in front of her would have contact with the diver, other than to hold the door for her. But on every mystery show she had seen, they always said you should watch for reactions when you asked questions.

"It was dreadful, all that barking. My babies were so

upset." The blonde pouted then took another sip of her drink and shuddered.

Amanda hesitated then clarified, "I meant the diver's death."

"Oh, yes, that too. We never met him, but so sad." Mrs. Erling paused. "What was your name again?"

"Amanda Warren, Pink Power Wash and Groom. Can I meet your pups?"

The blonde sat up and proudly plucked one of the dogs off the sofa. "This is Daisy; you can see she has a bit more curl to her hair." She kissed the top of Daisy's head and put her back on the sofa then picked up the other dog and rubbed her nose. "And this is Poppy. She's in charge."

Amanda hesitated. "Do they not like men?"

"Why would you ask that?"

"They reacted strongly to the skipper."

"Oh." Mrs. Erling shrugged. "They have never warmed up to him."

Amanda knelt next to the sofa and held out a hand. The curious dogs wandered closer. "When did you little beauties arrive in town?" Amanda asked the dogs but was pleased when Mrs. Erlings answered.

"Two days ago. It feels like forever."

"You were here in the marina when the diver was killed? That must have been scary. Did these girls wake you up barking?" Amanda asked the question directly to Mrs. Erling as she scratched the top of Daisy's head, and the dog leaned into the touch.

"Not during the night, but the next morning. We are visiting my husband's mother, and she was having an event at the Elysian Wave Lodge. Mrs. Erling invited everyone, even the crew." She shuddered. "It wasn't appropriate. You should have seen Cook's face when he saw the mayor there. Anyway, we've got rooms at the lodge, so we didn't have to return late. But Ocean Wood is so boring. Everyone just goes to bed in the evening and there is nothing to do, so I moved back onto the yacht." She picked a hair off her gown and sagged back into the cushion.

While Amanda mulled that over, she asked, "Can I give Poppy and Daisy treats?" She mentioned a healthy brand that was popular with her clients.

"Oh, no. They have a special diet. I'll have Mateo pack treats for you."

Amanda studied the well-manicured dogs, knowing this wouldn't take long, even with their double coats and special treatments. "You have their hair long, so they'll just need a light trim after their baths. It shouldn't take more than two hours."

The blonde rose from the couch and eyed Mateo. "Two hours... That will be enough time. Mateo will take care of what you need." Luna swept from the room without a backward glance.

Amanda studied her charges, and after letting them sniff her hands again, she tickled each of them under their chins. "We're going to have fun!"

She looked up at the blond man with the dark roots wiping down the kitchen. "Mateo, right? Do you have leashes?"

The handsome man left the galley area and, as he

brushed past her, gave her a smile that raised the heat on her cheeks.

Mateo opened a cabinet, and Amanda fanned herself as his back was to her. When he started pulling out what she would need, Amanda regained her composure enough to ask, "So, do you like living on a boat?"

"We're getting used to this smaller yacht. We previously had a crew of three. It's hard to downsize when the same level of service is required. But..." Mateo turned and gave her a wicked smile. "I always provide excellent service."

Amanda blinked. She had another question she wanted to ask, but she couldn't remember what it was for the life of her. Oh, right. "Why did they downsize?"

"I expect it was the beating the stock markets were taking. They cut our hours a few years ago, and the skipper and I started taking other jobs from December through April. We work together sometimes, mostly on the Caribbean and the Bahamas routes. The skipper is very in demand and takes outlier trips, like the Panama Canal, Japan, and some crazy places. I don't go with him on those. I'm happy to stay in the sun." Mateo cocked an eyebrow at her then ran his gaze from the top of Amanda's head, down her apron, to her sneaker-clad feet. He winked. "Here you go. Leashes and treats are in the bag. If you call me when you're done, I can buzz you in. Want my number?"

Amanda shook her head and blurted out, "No, th-thank you. I'm sure I'll be fine." She wanted to smack herself on the forehead; she might as well have said, "I carried a watermelon." She tried again. "They seem to travel a lot. Why come to Monterey?"

"We're up here a couple of times a year to visit Mr. Erling's mother, and the boss is also friends with your mayor."

That surprised Amanda, and she almost forgot to ask her last question. "So, did you also stay in the hotel two nights ago?"

"Yes, we all did. There was a mechanical issue with the yacht's AC system, and we were getting it repaired."

Amanda squinted, trying to remember Ben's mechanic's name. "Did you have it repaired by Mo?"

Mateo's flirty expression faded. "No. The skipper knew someone; he always has a resource. Why?"

"I was just wondering. My friend, Ben, is next to you, and he's having a lot of work done on his yacht, so I thought maybe he would like other repair options," Amanda said, making up a quick reason.

Mateo walked her out on the deck and grimaced as he looked over at Ben's vessel. "I'm not sure that qualifies as a yacht. It might not even qualify as a boat by the end of the day. At least he won't have to worry about anything being stolen."

Amanda followed his gaze and saw Ben's boat listing to one side. Tubing and cables hung off the sides like it was on life support. "What do you mean, stolen?"

"There have been a few break-ins around the marina. We're keeping the yacht locked up when we aren't here. Better to be safe."

Amanda hurried to follow Mateo down to the swim

platform and stepped onto the dock. Turning, she accepted each dog handed to her.

"You'll need to carry them. Mrs. Erling doesn't like them wandering the docks." Mateo loaded the bag with the rest of their gear in her arms, and Amanda staggered a little under the weight. "See you in two hours."

Mateo disappeared into the boat, and Amanda wondered what she had gotten herself into.

Minutes later, her hands full of squirming dogs, Amanda fumbled to open the marina gate. The bag of supplies fell to the ground, and as she struggled to pick it up, her purse slid off her shoulder. Squatting, she put the dogs down and dug around in the bag for their leashes.

Hearing footsteps, Amanda glanced up. Jack Roberts was walking down the dock away from the clubhouse. He looked around as if concerned someone was following.

Amanda looked in the direction he was heading, and a slight motion on one of the boats caught her attention. A tall, older man with long, light-colored hair was hiding on the boat Jack was approaching. The hidden man glanced up and caught Amanda's eye before he bolted deeper into the boat's interior. Another movement caught her eye, this one barely perceptible. She stared intently at the spot until she realized it was Grok crouched on the deck of a sailboat, watching the marina manager.

A sharp bark brought her back to the two dogs staring impatiently at her.

"Sorry, guys." Amanda snapped on their leashes and unlocked the gate, and then scooping up the bags, she shuffled herself and the dogs around the fenced door, leaving it to slam behind her. Off the dock now, the dogs sniffed their surroundings and squatted to stamp their mark on the territory.

Amanda looked over her shoulder. She really wanted to talk to Jack Roberts and find out about the thefts and when he last saw Tobias.

A tugging on the leashes brought her attention back to Daisy and Poppy. Their coats flowed around them as they walked. She would talk to the marina manager when her job here was done.

SEVENTEEN

Breakfast

Grok was serious when he said he was going to find breakfast, and that hunt had him following his nose along the side of the marina to the large clubhouse building. He managed to sneak in the door behind a young girl who said she was looking for her rowing class.

While the front desk staff hurried to help the girl find her group, Grok helped himself to the bowl of eggs and bacon they left unattended at the counter. Moving quickly, he finished the bowl. He was just cleaning his whiskers and admiring the view of the marina the full front windows gave him when he heard footsteps returning.

He made a quick strategic retreat through an opening into a shop.

"Who ate my food?" a woman said from behind him.

Grok crouched low and crawled under a low-hanging clothes rack. The arms of shirts and jackets fluttered around him. Startled, he stepped back, knocking over a stack of tiny T-shirts. Getting caught up in one, he ended half-in, half-out of the material. It flapped behind him as he bolted for the opening on the far side of the room.

"Hey, who knocked over the Grandma's Favorite Sailor display?" asked a raised voice behind him.

The next room was a small restaurant, but Grok was too concerned about the increased number of angry voices following him to stop and look for a second breakfast. He dove between a pair of legs, and the sound of breaking glass followed a shout.

Driven from the room, he jumped a barrier and found himself in a small seating area. The tall backs of the chairs temporarily blocked the view of the rest of the clubhouse. A small boat sat in a corner on a rubber mat, surrounded by children's toys. Covered in colorful stickers like the toys at the library had been, the brightly painted boat was full of squishy fake animals. Grok jumped into the boat and, giving a kick of his hind legs, ejected a dog-shaped animal and took its seat just as a group of people appeared behind the high-backed chairs.

"I thought I saw something come this direction." A young woman with her brown hair scraped back from her face picked the fake dog up from the floor and cuddled it as she studied the room. She searched for him for several minutes with the others, her face falling as they finally gave up and left.

Grok slumped from the pose he had held while they looked right at him.

Humans. Not so bright.

Deciding this was as good a place as any to nap, creepy

but comfortable, he settled deeper into the pile of fake animals and let the sun rays coming through the window do their work.

It was sometime later in the morning that Grok woke up feeling refreshed. Yawning, he slowly shook off sleep and looked around. He was still alone, but he could see everyone coming and going from the clubhouse to the docks. That's how he saw the marina manager, that male named Roberts, stop outside the clubhouse. He pulled a phone out of his pocket and looked at it before holding it to his ear. He scratched at his big belly while he talked on the phone. Then he glanced around and headed to the docks.

"That was shifty," Grok said to himself, allowing a tiny flicker of pleasure at using one of the new words he had picked up watching the TV box. "And I'm going to find out what he is up to."

Wading through the fake animals was harder than he expected. After stepping on several soft squishy faces and getting rolled under the herd once, he finally got his balance and could climb to the edge of the boat. His jump to the ground from there sent the boat rocking and the animals flying.

Escaping out an open window, he ran down the dock in time to see Roberts hold the door for a family exiting the marina. They insisted he go ahead, and he passed them while they held the door for the stragglers in their group. Grok got through behind a teen with her nose buried in a book.

When he caught up with Roberts, he was boarding a

silver-striped version of the big boat that was docked next to Ben's, this one all wrapped up in canvas like it was being stored. From the way Roberts was sneaking on, it definitely wasn't his.

A smaller boat across the way had a perfect view of the inside of the silver-striped boat. Grok settled onto its canvas cover deck and watched Roberts begin going through drawers. He also could see another male with long white hair coming up the inside steps. He snuck up on the manager, who spun, and the two males started shouting. The argument was short-lived. Roberts seemed to be demanding something from the white-haired male, and finally, he took an item out of a drawer and handed it to him. Roberts left after that.

Grok rolled onto his back and twisted against a bump in the deck, giving his back a good scratch. He wasn't sure what to make of this, maybe Amanda would have an idea.

EIGHTEEN

The Beast

Exactly two hours later, Amanda turned off the hair dryer and straightened to stretch her back. She lifted Poppy to the ground so she could keep working on a kink in Daisy's wavy strands. The Pekingese were beautiful clients. They love to be brushed and bathed. She was giving each of them a final trim when she heard scratching at the door.

Amanda slid open the RV door and was surprised to see Grok with a scowl on his face.

"Took you long enough. I was trapped in that marina for hours, waiting for someone to leave. Those gates are too high to jump." Grok hopped into the van and stalked over to his bowl. "Eh, this tastes worse than tap water."

"We don't have any more of the bottled type you like," Amanda explained.

Grok twitched his whiskers and eyed the bottle on the counter. "What's that?"

"That's for Poppy and Daisy." Amanda protested.

Grok just glared back at her. "Would you drink stale tank water?"

Amanda sighed. He had a point. The water in the RV's tank was safe to drink and wash the dogs, but it tasted funky. "Fine." She emptied Grok's bowl out the door and poured him fresh water from the bottle.

He was silent for several minutes as he drank, breathing a sigh of relief when he came up for air.

Grok flopped back onto his plush bed.

Something squawked under him, and the cat jumped vertically. Claws out on all four paws, he latched on to an apron hanging on a hook above his bed. He swung wildly, his weight threatening to tear the seams.

Amanda tried to choke back a laugh and snorted instead. Gasping, she leaned on the grooming table to hold herself up. Covering her mouth, she couldn't contain the second snort.

"It's not funny. What's that beast doing in my bed—" Grok let out a scream as the knot holding the apron on the hook gave way, and he plunged down.

Poppy let out an equally horrified yelp as she saw the cat falling towards her and scrambled off from the cushion so fast it shoved the bed across the room.

Grok landed, limbs spread, with a splat on the bare floor.

"Oh, Grok!" Amanda quickly unclipped Daisy's lead and set her on the floor before rushing to check on the cat.

Grok lay still. His voice muffled in the floor. "This has not been the best week for me."

"I thought cats always landed on their feet. Are you

hurt?" Amanda squatted beside the cat and ran her fingers down his spine to check for injuries.

"Just my pride." His voice muffled, Grok rolled onto his side.

When she saw that he was okay, she pats his head, tickling behind his ears as he liked, and then turned her attention to Poppy. The dog was fine and receiving comforting licks from her sister.

"So, what did you find out?" Amanda pushed the bed back near the cat.

While she cleaned up, Daisy and Poppy recovered from their shock, and both dogs sniffed curiously at the cat as they moved carefully toward him. Grok endured enough to satisfy their curiosity then hissed when they tried to take over his bed. The dogs lost interest and started sniffing the rest of the van.

"I learned that the marina manager is up to something," Grok still looked rattled when he lifted a paw and used it to start combing his mane.

"You know, I can help you with that." Grok ignored her as he had most of her past offers at grooming, so she carried on like she hadn't made the overture. "What did you see?"

"I was watching him from the clubhouse."

Amanda gave him a nod to continue as she finished wiping down the counter and started feeding towels into the laundry chute.

"He got a call and then started acting very shifty." Grok paused.

Amanda assumed it was so she could be impressed. She

hummed an acknowledgement. Satisfied, Grok switched paws as he told her what he had witnessed.

"Could you see what the man gave Roberts?" Amanda had stopped working and was watching him.

"I might be able to remember over lunch."

"It's not even noon." Amanda threw her hands up in the air—that cat.

"Just making sure you keep your priorities straight." Grok went to work on his back legs.

"I'm ready to take the dogs back. Are you coming with me?"

"No, I'll wait here. I've had enough wandering around the marina for a day."

Amanda funneled through Daisy's and Poppy's hair to snap rhinestone collars around their necks then attached the leashes and slid open the RV's door.

"I might be a few minutes. I want to try and talk to Jack and see if I can find out what he was up to. I also need to find out if he had an alibi for the murder." Amanda stepped out of the van and lifted each Pekingese out after her. She grabbed their bag of supplies.

"What did the fancy boat owners tell you?" Grok asked.

"I might be able to remember over lunch," Amanda shot back at the cat and received a hiss of displeasure as she slammed the door shut.

On the way back from dropping off the dogs with Mateo, Amanda detoured towards the clubhouse. She entered the building through the offices and tried to look casual as she glanced around, searching for Jack. The entry was set up as a sales area, showing off the marina services. A row of offices lined one wall, the other opened to a restaurant, and everything was designed to funnel you towards the floor-to-ceiling windows showing off the dock and boats and the view across the bay.

A young woman in a polo shirt with Ocean Wood Harbor Marina's logo bounced out of an office and beamed at Amanda. "Hi, I'm Sammy. Can I help you?"

"I'm looking for Jack Roberts." Amanda thought asking for him would speed things up instead of just pretending to bump into him. She was running out of time if she and Grok wanted to get lunch before their next appointment.

"The marina manager is very busy. We've got an upcoming race this weekend. We sponsor many of them throughout the year. Is there something I can help you with?" The woman's ponytail bounced as she spoke.

"I was thinking about becoming a member of the club, but I was definitely told to talk to Jack about it. Does he have a couple of minutes?" Amanda thought that sounded plausible.

"Let me see." The young woman disappeared and re-emerged with Jack trailing behind her. His big smile slid to confusion as he saw Amanda.

She stepped forward and held out a hand. "I don't think we got introduced yesterday. I'm Amanda Warren."

Frowning, he shook her hand. "Jack Roberts, Ocean Wood Harbor Marina Manager."

"I heard you lived on your boat here, the same as my friend Ben."

"Mmhmm." Jack tipped his head to the side and narrowed his eyes. "I thought you wanted to ask about membership?"

"Oh, yes, but I don't have a boat." Amanda wasn't sure it was a good idea to admit that. She was surprised by Jack's response.

"That's not a problem. We have a lot of members without boats. Some people like to take our sailing classes. Others enjoy our clubhouse dinners. You might not know it, but we have a wide list of members, even celebrities." Jack went on to explain how membership worked.

"I heard someone mention speargun fishing. Is that something I could learn here? Do you spearfish?" She wasn't sure exactly what type of equipment it would require but assumed the gun and bolts would be needed.

Jack frowned. "No, we don't offer that."

"So, you don't have any of the equipment here?" Amanda added.

"Why do you want to know about that?" Jack gave her a suspicious look.

Amanda tried to backpedal. "Well, when I met you yesterday morning, you said someone had been stealing from the marina. And then we heard about a diver being killed with a speargun, and I worried thieves were running around the marina with guns. It made me very nervous. I should have just come out and asked you about it." It wasn't a lie. Amanda *was* worried about a killer with a speargun.

"The theft was just a couple of fishing rods. Nothing dangerous," Jack assured her.

Amanda placed her hand across her chest. "Well, it is a relief to know that no one around here has a speargun."

"Now, I didn't say that. Spearfishing is legal, and most people do it right. But the marina is a very safe environment for our clients and their boats."

"Did Tobias have a speargun?" Amanda asked.

"I don't know what the divers keep in their dock boxes, and only the police know what killed Tobias. Are you interested in joining or not?" The marina manager put his hands on his hips and scowled down at Amanda.

"I am, but I'd like to talk to the sailing instructor if I could since I'm most interested in taking lessons. Is she available?"

"She works afternoon and evenings. You can stop in and visit her later."

Amanda decided to try a hunch. "That's right. She was working late the evening Tobias was killed."

"How did you know that?" Jack paced the small showroom.

"I met her the next morning, and she must have mentioned it. Wow. That would have been a long day for her. How late did she work?"

"It was a bit of a surprise when she volunteered to clean out the rental returns. I couldn't get to them, and we needed them for the next day." Jack cut himself off. "Why are you asking all these questions?"

Amanda blinked, stalling as she tried to come up with a reason.

"Look, I need to go. Sammy here can help you with any other questions you have."

Jack bolted. The young woman frozen behind the counter gave Amanda a deer-in-headlights look.

Round-eyed, Amanda stared back then shook herself. "I think I have everything I need for now. I'll stop in and talk to Robin later." After an awkward wave, Amanda left the club.

She had learned some interesting information there but couldn't figure out how it fit with everything else. Shouldn't she have had a stroke of genius or an epiphany and know who the killer was? Maybe she wasn't very good at this. Maybe she should let the police do their job, as the chief was fond of telling her. But then Amanda thought about losing Ben, and she knew she couldn't just leave his name being cleared to chance. As she walked down the ramp, her knees were trembling. And maybe she needed lunch.

NINETEEN

Booby Trap

When Amanda returned to her sister's house, the back of her neck prickled as she stepped onto the front porch. Was someone watching her?

"Grok, do you feel—"

The gray cat's ears were twitching as the hair on his neck rose. "You check inside. I'll look around out here."

Grok slinked into the bushes and disappeared. Amanda took a quick second to marvel how such a large cat could be so stealthy before attempting to mimic his covert grace herself. She softly stepped towards the front door, cringing as she dragged her shoes against the gravel and broke a very loud twig.

Cautiously entering the house, she debated locking the door behind her. *Was it better to have it open so she could run screaming out or locked so no one could enter behind her?* In the end, she compromised, leaving the door open but dragging a low shoe rack from the closet to block the entrance. She could jump it if she had to escape.

In the closet with the shoe rack, Amanda found a stout stick, the kind the police carried in those British mysteries. Holding it in both hands like a baseball bat, she walked around the house, pushing open doors and looking behind furniture. She ended in the kitchen, not having found anything different from when they had left in a rush that morning.

Had she imagined the feeling of eyes on her? No, Grok had noticed it too.

While she waited for the cat to return from scoping the area, Amanda started lunch.

She made a sandwich for herself and put out a can of tuna, which Grok would turn his nose up at but still eat when she wasn't looking. She pulled out the schedule to check her appointments for the rest of the day while she waited for him.

Most of her clients, especially the older ones, wanted home visits that were scheduled in advance, but she tried to keep a couple of afternoons a week open for people who wanted a quick cut or to drop off their pets.

A crash sounded from the front of the house.

Amanda jumped to her feet and grabbing her stick, headed for the sound.

By the front door, the shoe rack had toppled over and the entryway was a pile of shoes.

Grok's head was in a boot on the floor, and his back legs were caught up in the rack. An espadrille wedge whipped through the air as he kicked furiously to detangle from the lace.

"Grok, are you okay?" Amanda grabbed the wedge and then pulled the shoe rack off the shelf.

A hissing growl had Amanda stepping back.

"Free me."

"Hold still," Amanda instructed as she reached out a tentative hand and pulled on the boot, Grok's head popped free like a cork.

"You're okay. You walked into my booby trap."

"What?" The cat flipped to his feet, the lace unwinding from his leg as Amanda held the shoe. Grok shook his head and surveyed the scene. "I thought these were shoes... What's a booby?"

"That's a, well—" Amanda cut off as Grok shook his head.

"Never mind." The cat stalked off to the kitchen.

Amanda wanted to talk to Grok about what he had seen at the marina that morning, but the cat looked pretty miffed and not in the mood to share.

Soon Amanda's first client arrived at Alexandra's house, with a steady stream keeping her occupied until it was time to meet Ben at the coffee shop to hand off Qbert so he could attend a meeting.

They had set the appointment up a few days ago, but with everything that had happened, she hadn't been able to confirm, so she texted Ben while she placed their order at the Bean & Book shop.

We're here.

Grabbing their drinks, she settled at a table by the window and waited for Ben to arrive.

"I think the manager demanded cash from the white-haired male this morning."

"Oh, now you want to talk to me?" Amanda glanced around then frowned at the cat. "Wait, did you say cash? Are you sure?"

"I might be a cat, but I know what money is." Grok eyed the neighbor's latte with a hungry look.

Amanda pushed the cat's bowl of milk closer to him, "Why would he give him cash?"

"Could he be paying for something?"

"Like rent, for the boat slip? Maybe, but most people would just transfer the money electronically or write a check. Why would—" She stifled what she was going to add as someone passed close to their table, and then she shook her head to Grok and hoped he understood they would have to finish the conversation later.

The café grew crowded as more customers came in for their afternoon coffee fix.

Where was Ben? He was very late. Maybe he'd decided to take Qbert to his meeting.

Someone bumped their table.

Amanda grabbed her drink as she looked up and called out, "Hello!"

Robin McArthur turned around; her freckled brow crinkled. "Do I know—oh, you were at the marina when they found..."

"Yes. I'm Amanda Warren. I'm so sorry for your loss."

"It's all wrong." Robin McArthur stared down at her shoes, and a shudder ran through her.

While Amanda wondered what she meant, the barista announced Robin's name.

"You're welcome to join us." Amanda's voice was gentle as she pushed Grok off the chair and moved her coffee cup aside.

Robin nodded and went to fetch her coffee. When she returned, she took the chair across from Amanda and wrapped her hands around the cup, staring into the dark liquid.

"Were you and Tobias close?" Amanda inquired.

The other woman shrugged, sandy blonde hair falling into her face. "Not especially. I mean, we worked long hours together. It's a small crew at the marina, so when there is an event or a class, things could get intense. Safety is important, and you have to be vigilant." She clenched her mug.

Amanda raised an eyebrow. "Tobias didn't pay attention at work?"

"I didn't mean that. He was a good worker, but he got caught up in his side projects. It's easy to do in our industry. When you're on a job, you work long hours, flat out, and then in between gigs, you pick up bits of work here and there. That's why I took the instructor position. Wanted a little bit more stability while I was in Ocean Wood."

"You're not from the Monterey area?"

"Nah. Started working boats in Tasmania, made my way through Southeast Asia, Africa, Europe, the Mediterranean, the Caribbean..." The lines in Robin's face eased, and her eyes took on a dreamy look. "I'm a citizen of the sea."

"That sounds amazing." Amanda thought about her own road trip to California and how freeing—but also scary—it had been to pick her own path. "Don't you get lonely?"

"Sometimes. But you meet a lot of interesting people along the way." Robin's voice took on a lyrical tone as she quoted, "I'd rather be a shooting star that lights up the night than a distant planet that drifts in darkness."

Amanda ignored the sound of the cat pretending to cough up a furball at her feet "Was that a quote from someone?"

"Everett Sage, in his 18th century book *Philosophy of the Tides*. It's very good, if you can find a translated version."

"I'll look for it." Amanda winced as a claw sank into her ankle.

As Robin drained the rest of her coffee, Amanda shook her leg free of Grok and looked down at the phone. No messages. Ben should be deep into his meeting by now. He must not be coming. She should probably head back to the house and clean the RV and prep it for tomorrow. Grok was definitely ready to leave.

Robin stood. "Thanks for sharing the table. I need to take off. Jack refuses to cancel the regatta next week, says there is too much money at stake."

"For a race?"

"Sure. A lot of competitors are coming into town. The marina will start filling up this weekend and it will get busy, so I'm going out this afternoon to check a section of the path and navigation instructions for the competitors."

Amanda's breath spiked. Could Tobias have been killed because he caught a team breaking in? Would one team sabotage another? "Robin, would having that information in advance give a team an edge in the race?"

"No. The teams need to know the route in advance. It's how they deal with the conditions and the other competitors that make the race fun. Look, I need to go while the wind is still good."

"That sounds so much better than my plans." Amanda couldn't help thinking of the furball wrangling and slobber mopping ahead of her. "I have more questions about the race. Can we talk again?"

"Sure, but why don't you come with me? Then you can ask your questions while I work."

"On the boat?" A thrill of nerves and temptation swept through Amanda's belly. "I've never been on a sailboat before. Don't I have to know how to be a crew member or something?"

"I could do it on my own. It would just be good to have the company. I'll explain how the race works as we go. We should only be an hour."

Amanda checked her texts again. Ben hadn't responded to any of her messages or the voicemail she had left him. He must not be coming. She had finished her appointments for the day, compressing them all, thinking she'd be watching Qbert. She couldn't pass up this opportunity to question Robin more.

Tugging at a strand of curly red hair that had escaped

the elastic band, she agreed. "Okay, I'd love to go if you don't mind a novice. Are you sure we'll only be an hour?"

"Yeah, got an early dinner appointment I need to be back for, so we can't be longer than that." Robin turned and hurried towards the door.

Amanda stuck her head under the table, pretending to collect her purse. "Grok, are you coming?"

The cat tilted his head. "Are you crazy? How do you know she isn't the killer?"

Amanda laughed. "She's not. I was with her when she found out about Tobias. She was shocked, and she told Detective Kim her alibi."

"If you say so. But I'm not risking it. Besides, she smells funny, like coconut. I can't remember why that is important." Grok's voice trailed off.

Amanda was about to ask what he meant when he added. "I'm going to stay and follow the marina manager again to see what more I learn. If you don't come back, I can tell them to look in the bay for your body."

Amanda blinked rapidly then pressed her hands to her ear. "I'm not listening to you. You're just trying to psych me out."

"I don't even know what that means," Grok called over his shoulder as he left.

Amanda tried to shake the sudden onset of nerves from Grok's comments and quickly left the coffee shop to catch up with Robin, chanting under her breath. "It's going to be okay. I love canoeing. How much harder can this be?"

TWENTY

Whale of a Time

Before she knew it, Robin had Amanda in a life vest and they were on a boat, sailing out of the harbor entrance towards the breakwater. They passed a whale-watching boat returning to the dock, and a chorus of sea lions barked as they glided by.

"Sounds like they're greeting you!" Amanda called over the wind.

The other woman shook her head. "They're a menace. A sea lion will take over any dock they want, and you don't want to know what they'll do in your boat if they get on it."

Robin stood tall at the helm. Her sun-lightened blonde hair gently waved behind her and never seemed to get in her face. Dressed in shorts and a windbreaker with comfortable-looking white-soled shoes, she looked born to this life.

Amanda was braced, hunched over on the deck trying to keep her balance as she blinked into the wind and spit out strands of frizzy red hair that had slipped from her ponytail and were slapping her face. She tried retying her hair and managed a messier bun.

"You need a hat," Robin called out to her.

Amanda grunted in acknowledgment.

"Check the seat storage. I usually keep a spare in there."

Amanda made her way over to the seats behind the helm and pulled on the cushions on the left. They were stiff but slowly started to rise. Under the seat, she found a bucket, some tools, a blue bag with a white wave-shaped logo, the ink cracked in the middle, but no hat.

"No, not there." Robin's voice was sharp in the biting wind. She slammed shut the lid of the storage and lifted the cushions on the right side, pulling out an old white hat with a stiff brim and a strap.

Amanda pulled it on and tucked her hair underneath, sighing with relief.

As they cleared the marina, Robin did some captainy things that Amanda couldn't identify. Soon they were out in the open Monterey Bay. The sails opened up, and the boat started to fly.

"Are you sure there's nothing you need me to do?" Amanda called out. It was a little easier to talk now.

"Nope, I'm just checking the navigation marks. Why don't you tell me what brought you to Ocean Wood?" Robin ticked off something with a pencil on a notepad she had said was waterproof.

"My sister lives...lived here. We had grown apart." Amanda's chest ached, and she rubbed at the spot. "When

I left Ohio, I decided to reconnect. But by the time I got here, she was missing. I'm still trying to find her."

"That's a shame. Family is important." Robin changed course.

"Did Tobias have any family?" Amanda gripped the metal wire that circled the boat as the waves rocked them.

"I think he had a little brother." Robin nodded to a seat close to where she was navigating. "Why don't you sit here; it will be a little steadier for you."

"I could check off your list for you."

Robin chuckled. "No, that's not a good idea. You don't want to be reading your first time sailing. Look off to the starboard," she called, pointing to the right. "It's a humpback whale."

Amanda spun in her seat as a spray of water shot up a dozen yards away, and a gray hump slid through the water. A second later, a tail shot up covered in white barnacles, and then, with a huge splash, it disappeared into the inky gray waves. "Did you see that?" She clapped her hands as she jumped up.

"Steady there." Robin laughed. "It never gets old watching people see their first whale."

Amanda kept her eyes glued on the water, looking for more whales, as she asked, "Were you at the marina when Tobias was killed?"

"I was with Jack. We were working late strategizing the course for the race. I could've saved him." Robin stared off at the horizon.

What? A shiver raced down Amanda's spine. She shook her head in disbelief. Jack had said Robin was handling the rental returns alone that night. Someone was lying. But who? Standing on the boat, the water of the bay lapping around her, a horrifying thought struck her: was she trapped here with a killer?

As the boat slowly made its way back to the marina, Amanda's tension mounted with each minute. Doubt and suspicion clouded her thoughts, and she kept a wary eye on Robin, who navigated with eerie composure. By the time they neared the dock, Amanda was not only physically unsteady but mentally exhausted, eager to escape the confines of the boat and put some space between herself and Robin.

True to her promise, Robin docked the boat at the marina in just under an hour from when they left. As Amanda stepped off the sailboat, her legs wobbled slightly, still unsteady from the sea's sway. She watched Robin tie off the last knot.

"Well, thanks for answering my questions."

"Thanks for keeping me company. That was—" Robin seemed at a loss to describe the tension that had descended on their short trip "—nice." She offered a casual wave as she left, heading towards the clubhouse.

As Amanda started to follow, a sudden movement near Ben's boat caught her eye. She spotted Ben's familiar dark hair. With her heart lifting at the sight of a friendly face, she changed course, her steps leading her towards Ben instead. Her mind buzzed with questions and concerns, and she hoped Ben could provide some much-needed clarity.

TWENTY-ONE

Electric Sandwich

Amanda had never seen Ben so upset before. He stomped around the cabin of his little boat, slamming doors that bounced back open, moving plastic boxes and towels and then putting them back in their original location. He dropped a bucket full of water, and it splashed up the sides, dousing his face. Grabbing a dirty towel off a toolbox, he swiped at the water. "I can't believe you went sailing instead of watching Qbert."

"I waited for you and you didn't show. I texted, called... You didn't answer your phone. I thought you weren't coming."

"The morning meeting ran late, so this regroup meeting was delayed, and then I was running late, very late. When I got to the coffee shop, you weren't there, and I'd left my phone in my office so I couldn't call. I had to take Qbert with me to city hall. What a disaster."

Ben twisted the towel. "Qbert barked at my boss, who dropped his coffee on Chief Rodriguez's laptop. And that was just as we arrived. When he ate an important lab report, I finally had the assistant take him out. She was busy, so she locked him in the mayor's private bathroom so we could finish the meeting in peace. Qbert didn't like that and dislodged a roll of paper into the toilets, flooding the first floor and triggering an evacuation."

Amanda grabbed Ben's arm as she bit back a bark of laughter and wheezed, "Oh, Ben. Where's Qbert now?"

Ben sank into the cushioned seat of the dinette. "Dottie and Albert were at city hall. She laughed so hard, she said she peed herself. They took Qbert. Claimed their grandkids were visiting and he could keep them occupied. I think they just made that up because they felt bad for me. This has all been a disaster."

Amanda shifted from foot to foot, trying to keep balanced with the boat's gentle rocking. At least the vessel wasn't listing to the side anymore. "I'm so sorry. If I thought you were coming, I never would have gone sailing."

Ben shook his head. "It's not your fault. I'm just frustrated. I got officially put on administrative leave today. Said I was too distracted." Ben ran his hands through his hair, clutching at the ends before dropping to his elbows on the table.

"I'm sorry. They're missing out by not having you on the case." Amanda slid into the seat across from him.

"Not their fault. I understand it's protocol. They can't clear me as a suspect, so I can't be anywhere near this or any other cases. I'm just so frustrated about the boat, and I'm wondering why I'm still here."

"You mean in Monterey? Are you really thinking of leaving?"

"Maybe," Ben sighed and put his head down on the table.

"Do you know what's wrong with her?" Amanda had been wondering but was afraid to ask.

"Everything. As far as I can tell, almost everything is wrong with this boat. I should have gotten an inspection. It looked okay, and it was floating. The price was fantastic. Now I know why. I might have made a mistake here."

Someone knocked on the outside frame of the boat. "Ahoy in there?"

Amanda and Ben glanced up. The man standing outside looked familiar. He had curly silver hair and a wide-brimmed hat. Then she recognized him. This was the man she and Grok saw this morning hiding on the boat and talking with the manager.

Amanda went out to greet him. "Hello... Do I know you?"

"Well, if you don't, you may be the only person in town." The man laughed loudly then glanced around before shrugging.

Ben joined them on deck, excitement in his voice as he blurted out, "You're Silver—Carlos Silva, the head singer for the Electric Sandwich Band. I love your music." Ben lunged across the space to shake the older man's hand, pumping it up and down enthusiastically until Amanda put a hand on his arm to stop him from dragging the man onto the boat.

"Would you like to come aboard?" Amanda swept her arm wide.

Silver looked back over his shoulder again. "Maybe that would be better. You never know who is watching with a long lens."

Amanda stepped back. As the musician passed, she noticed the sweet, spicy smell of whiskey. Ben led the man into the cabin, moving several buckets so the three of them could sit at the dinette. "What can we do for you?"

Up close, Amanda could tell the musician was in his early seventies, yet he exuded the youthful energy of a man many years his junior. Maybe it was the way he dressed and that his physique remained lean. But you could see his age in the laugh lines that creased his eyes.

"I'm sorry I can't offer you a drink. As you can tell, everything is a bit of a mess right now."

The musician waved his hand. "Already had a drink. I'm here to ask a favor. I find myself in a bit of a bind," he confessed, his voice low and earnest as he turned to Amanda. "After you saw me this morning, I knew I needed to appeal to you to not reveal my location. You see, my fans think I'm at my home in Stone Beach working on my next tour, not bobbing on the waves. If they knew the truth, if they knew I was here, they would storm this place." His plea hung in the salty sea air.

Amanda remembered seeing Silver hiding on a boat from Jack. Grok said the men argued then Jack accepted something from this man. There was more to this then just avoiding fans but explaining that would require her confession that she had received information from a talking cat. She didn't think that would go over well.

"Why doesn't management tighten security so you're safer here?" Not that increased security wouldn't deter a murderer on the loose.

Silver flinched. "I really need your help, so I'm going to come clean. Management won't give me liveaboard permission. Security would be a nightmare and expensive. My wife kicked me out, and after all those years on the road, I hate staying in hotels. So, I'm a stowaway, living on my own boat. I've been sneaking in and out so the tabloids and management don't see me. I just don't want the newspapers to know." Silver's pleading smile transformed his face, and his presence was mesmerizing.

Amanda could see why he was a popular figure. "I'm not a reporter, and I don't plan on talking to one."

"Me neither." Ben shook his head. "Your secret is safe with us."

The musician relaxed and gave a big sigh. "Thank you, I appreciate it. We should drink on it." He looked around. "Maybe another time. Over at my boat."

Amanda's spine stiffened. "I just realized, since you've been sneaking around while you stayed here, maybe you can tell us if you've seen anything unusual happening."

"What do you mean by unusual?" Silver leaned back in the seat, the vinyl creaking beneath him.

Amanda tapped a finger to her lips. "Well, people sneaking around who shouldn't be here? Boats broken into. Items missing?"

Silver nodded. "That sailing instructor skulks around

at night a lot. I've seen her sneaking on and off boats and caught her trying to get onto my yacht once. It looked like she was searching for something. Oh, and Jack snuck on my boat once he figured out what I was up to. But I bribed him not to tell anybody I was here."

Amanda could feel Ben bristling beside her. "That explains why it took so long for me to get help in my boat. I didn't think to bribe him. Not that I would have."

"Where were you two nights ago at midnight?" Amanda asked.

Ben made a tutting sound behind her.

Silver tugged on his ear as he thought about it, and then his face lit up. "Oh, that's when Jack and I came to an understanding. I gave him the first payment, and then we got to talking and drinking. We might have had a few too many. Neither of us were walking around much after that. I went below deck to bed around one a.m. Left him snoozing on the dinette. Not sure when he headed back to his boat."

"Do you always have drinks with your blackmailers?" Ben shifted in his seat.

"It gets lonely here at night. Sometimes it's nice to have someone to drink with, even if they're taking bribes or selling your information to the paparazzi." Silver gave a smile that didn't reach his eyes.

Amanda felt a little sad for the rock star but wondered if he was telling the truth this time. If Silver was drinking with and paying off Jack, that explained why the manager lied about his alibi. But it also confirmed Robin didn't have an alibi. She needed to get to Detective Kim and let him know.

TWENTY-TWO

Crunch

When Grok finally found Amanda, she was hurrying across the marina towards the gate. Quickly traversing the docks, he jumped on dock boxes and boats, loving how they swayed beneath him to speed his progress.

He gave a loud growl.

In the process of going through the chain link gate, Amanda spun around, catching the door before it could slam in the cat's face. "I thought you were still at the coffee shop."

Grok padded along next to Amanda, keeping pace as she hurried to the RV. "No, I wanted to check what the manager has been up to."

Amanda interrupted him. "You were right."

Grok smirked. "Of course I was. What was I right about?"

"The sailing instructor, Robin, lied to the police about her alibi. She told me she was with Jack, but Jack said he was alone. Then I found out he was hiding, that he was really with Silver, but we can't tell anyone that."

"Who is Silver?"

"That doesn't matter since we can't mention it anyway. The important part is that Robin doesn't have an alibi and she has been sneaking around the boats. Which I suppose doesn't make her the killer, but it is suspicious. I can't believe I was just out in the open water with her; she could have dumped me overboard at any time!" Amanda shuddered and dropped the keys she had just dug out of her purse. "I tried to call Detective Kim. He isn't answering his phone, so I'm heading over there now. I'm sure when he hears this, they will clear Ben to work and he won't go back to San Francisco."

"So, he's still planning on leaving?"

"Yes." Amanda scooped up her keys and unlocked the door.

"Hurry, get in." She shooed him into the van.

Grok bristled. He didn't like being rushed. He rubbed his tail against Amanda's face as she tried to push him along. As soon as he jumped into the passenger seat, Amanda climbed into the vehicle behind him. She slammed the door and started the engine, fumbling with her seat belt as she headed to the exit.

They were out on the street driving towards the town center in no time. When Amanda took the corner way too fast, Grok flew forward, splatting against the windshield like one of those orange cat window clings.

"Watch it," Grok complained as he jumped back into

the seat and tucked himself under the seat belt Amanda left buckled for him.

"Sorry, Grok. I didn't realize I was going that fast." She pushed on the brake, but nothing happened. Amanda stood, pressing the brake pedal with her foot. They didn't slow. "Something is wrong with the van."

Grok watched as Amanda gripped the steering wheel with both hands. Her eyes were wide as she approached the next corner. She pushed at the floor, but the vehicle didn't slow.

"Watch out for the car!" Grok yelled and burrowed deeper into the seat, his nails digging into the upholstery.

"I'm trying. The brakes aren't working. I can't slow down." Amanda's swerve around a car forced her to take the corner.

Grok's claws slashed the upholstery as he slid. Two wheels of the vehicle started to lift from the ground.

Grok squawked.

Amanda screamed.

There was a crunching sound, and the van suddenly stopped.

"Are you okay?" Amanda reached out toward Grok.

Was he? Grok sheathed his claws and took a moment to assess how he felt. Nothing was broken. His head hurt from hitting the windshield earlier, but the seat belt had helped restrain him in the crash.

"Grok, hello? I asked if you were okay." Amanda undid her belt and leveraged herself from her seat; leaning over him, she ran a hand over his fur as if to ensure he was all right.

Grok shrugged her off. "I'm okay. How about you?"

Amanda sank back into the seat. "I'm going to be sore tomorrow. I need to check if anyone was hurt. I just can't breathe yet."

Strands of red hair had escaped the nest on Amanda's head and covered one eye as she wrung her hands. Grok couldn't tell if she was checking for injuries or working up the nerve to call the police.

There was a knock at the driver's door. Amanda and Grok spun towards the sound and saw Chief Rodriguez's angry face framed in the window.

It occurred to Grok that he should look at what they had hit. Putting two front paws on the dashboard, he looked down the hood to see the police cruiser that had stopped their momentum.

TWENTY-THREE

Dead Wake

Amanda couldn't believe she had crashed into the car of the person who liked her the least in all of Ocean Wood. If not for the seat belt–shaped bruise forming on her chest, she would have rested her head on the steering wheel and surrendered to the police. Since arriving in town, her only fault, besides finding several dead bodies, was looking exactly like the chief's missing best friend. And for that, the chief had taken an immediate dislike to her. Maybe it wasn't all about her. Detective Kim had said it was the "memories you evoke," so there must be a story behind the police partners' split and why her sister had ended up a PI. But right now, with Chief Gina Rodriquez shining her I'm-going-to-murder-you eyes at Amanda, the *why* didn't matter as much as the *how*, as in, *how am I going to get out of this.*

There was another tap at the window. Amanda pushed the button to lower it, but nothing happened, so she cracked the door.

"Anyone hurt?" Rodriguez's tone was sharp as she peered into the RV to assess the situation for herself. Detective Kim hovered behind her.

Amanda shook her head and winced as a wave of pain shot through her at the motion. "No. A bit rattled, but no injuries. Is everyone in your car, okay?"

"Detective Kim might have a little whiplash, but we're fine. How about the cat? Is he okay?"

Amanda confirmed that Grok was indeed unbroken but not likely to forgive her anytime soon.

As soon as the chief received Amanda's confirmation, the concerned, professional officer from minutes before was gone. "You were driving completely out of control. Do you have any excuse for your behavior?" She didn't wait for an answer. Spittle flew from her mouth as she pointed a finger at Amanda, and her voice rose to a level the whole town could hear. "You're lucky you just hit a car. You could have killed someone. You could have died yourself. What were you thinking?"

Grok hissed at the chief, swiping out a paw and causing the dark-haired woman to step back.

Amanda slid out of the RV. Holding on to the door frame, she stood on shaky legs and tried to organize her thoughts. "Something's wrong with my brakes."

"What do you mean?" The detective edged in front of the chief, separating the women.

"They worked fine this morning, but when I used them the first time leaving the parking lot, they felt spongy, soft. Then when I tried to brake the second time, nothing happened."

"When did you last get them replaced?" Kim frowned.

Amanda shook her head. "They've been working fine. I think someone tampered with them."

"Seriously? You're going to pretend this wasn't your fault? Why would someone bother tampering with your brakes?" The dark-haired woman's face was turning red. On her cheek was a cut, and a bruise was starting to form around it.

Detective Kim stepped back and tried to lean down and look under the RV. He winced as he stood, rubbing a hand over his chest. His impeccable suit had a coffee stain down the front. "Why do you think your brakes were tampered with?"

Chief Rodriguez interrupted the detective. "It was your lack of maintenance and recklessness that caused this accident. Where were you speeding to?"

"I was coming to see him." Amanda pointed to Detective Kim.

The detective's brows rose, and he waited for Amanda to explain.

Clutching her purse, she glanced from the chief back to the detective. "I'm sure it can wait."

The I'm-going-to-murder-you glare was back.

Around them, officers checked the vehicles for gas spills, and others cordoned off the street to keep anyone else from becoming involved and creating a pile-up. It looked like a full-on crime scene. Several other police cars arrived with screaming sirens, and the fire department and paramedics were just pulling up. Most of Ocean Wood's population stood on the sidewalk watching the show.

Limbs still twitching with shock, Amanda held on to the RV door and watched the scene unfold. Everything was being done with military precision.

Chief Rodriguez narrowed her eyes. When she spoke, her voice sounded nasally, and she rubbed at her nose as she questioned Amanda like a suspect. "It was important enough for you to rush here."

Amanda sighed then gave in and told the officers her suspicions about Robin McArthur.

The chief's eyebrows shot up to her hairline, and her voice reached supersonic level as she yelled, "Are you investigating?"

Amanda tugged at the strands of curly red hair that had escaped her bun in the crash. She tucked them behind her ears while she considered her options. How did she answer that without incriminating herself? Could she say she had been joking? Could she pretend she had amnesia and didn't know what was happening? Was that a thing, or was it just in movies? She should research that and see if any symptoms fit for Grok.

A shout came from the crowd.

Ben ran to her side. "Amanda, I heard the crash from the marina. I couldn't believe it when someone said a pink van was involved." He held up a hand, put his other hand on his knee, and bent over, panting. After several deep breaths, he stood but continued to hold his side. "Are you hurt?" He eyed Amanda and the chief's postures.

"I'm fine." Amanda grabbed on to the subject change.

Detective Kim motioned over an officer as he told Ben, "We're all fine. But the paramedics are recommending we go to the hospital to be checked over. Maybe the cat should go to the vet?"

At the mention of a doctor's visit, Grok started backing away from the group. "That quack's not poking in my head again."

"I'm not going anywhere until we find out what is happening here." Chief Rodriguez winced as she straightened and pushed her shoulders back.

Detective Kim gave his boss a measured look. "Ma'am, that isn't our job. This officer will take statements from each of you, and then we can go. I've already spoken with him." He indicated the man in the black uniform who was standing respectfully back from the group. "Ben, I'm going to leave Amanda in your hands while I check the rest of the scene."

As Amanda waited for her turn to talk to the officer, she caught a flash of fur as Grok wove between the working officers' feet. As soon as he was clear of the scene, he took off running towards home.

Several hours later, the sun was setting. The scene was finally cleared, and traffic flowed again. Both Chief Rodriguez and Amanda declined medical care.

A tow truck driver gave Amanda a form to sign. "Can you take it to the parking lot behind the travel agency building?" Maybe if it was there, she could still use it for grooming while she tried to come up with the money for repairs.

Detective Kim stopped the driver. "No. Take it to the police lot."

"What? I told you it wasn't my fault." Amanda threw up her hands.

Detective Kim gave her a steady look. "We found evidence that someone did tamper with your brakes. We just need a little time to learn the full extent of what happened."

Suddenly, all the adrenaline she had been running on disappeared, and Amanda sagged into Ben's side.

"Let me retrieve my car from the marina, and we can get some food. Then I'll take you home." Ben squeezed her shoulder.

"Take-out, please. I don't think I have enough left in me to sit at a table. I just want to curl up under a blanket."

"You stay here. I'll be right back with my car."

Suddenly, Amanda didn't want to be left alone. She felt too vulnerable. The street was emptying, and the light breeze blowing had turned chilly as the sun set. "I'll go with you. I don't want to stay here."

They walked the first few blocks in silence. A vibrant sunset peaked between houses, turning the ocean shades of glimmery oranges and reds. Trees became dark shapes against the sky.

"Why would someone tamper with my brakes? Were they trying to hurt us?" Amanda shivered and grabbed Ben's arm as she looked around the empty streets.

"Us?" Ben tugged on her jacket sleeve as she weaved too close to the curb.

"Grok and me." She didn't see Ben's frown as she stepped off the sidewalk and into the road to skirt a car parked half in the street.

"Who would have a reason to mess with your brakes?" Ben pulled her across the street as the sidewalk disappeared on one side and turned up on the other.

"That's what I don't know."

"After our conversation with Silver, you said you had to find Detective Kim. You took off without explaining why."

"Robin lied about her alibi, and she was sneaking onto boats. There's something going on with her."

"But you don't have any evidence or motive. The police are never going to take you seriously without any proof. And don't you think they would have checked the alibis and known that someone was lying?" Ben turned into the marina parking lot.

"I thought so, but it didn't look like Detective Kim knew about Jack being with Silver. What if Robin knew I was on to something and tampered with my brakes?" Amanda stopped beside Ben's car.

"But she was with you most of the afternoon. When would she have had time to do that?" Ben searched his pockets then planted a palm against his forehead. "I forgot. I have to go to the boat to get my keys. They're with the dog leash. Do you want to come with me?"

Amanda looked around the dark parking lot. "Sure. Maybe I can get something to drink?"

"I've got plenty of water."

"Bottled water," Amanda clarified.

With a chuckle, Ben led the way.

As they threaded through the docks, the sun disappeared on the ocean's horizon, leaving a sunset of colors reflecting off the water and turning the white boats sherbet orange. The light quickly faded, and the shapes on the dock became menacing shadows.

Amanda yelped as someone slammed a door. "It's spooky out here in the evenings."

"You're still in shock from the accident. A surprise like that can intensify your emotions and raise your blood pressure."

Amanda shuddered and tried to calm her breathing. "You may be right. I think I'm seeing things. Like, that boat, the one covered in a tarp, looks like a sleeping dragon. And that other one with the lumps, those look like huge men in capes, I keep expecting them to jump out at me."

Ben squinted in the direction she pointed.

"And look at your boat." She rubbed at her eyes. "There's a giant starfish on the bow."

"A what?"

"A starfish. See the head, the hands, the feet—why is the starfish barefoot?" Amanda drew closer.

"Amanda, that isn't a starfish." Ben stiffened beside her and fumbled in his pocket.

A pull in Amanda's gut yanked her closer, closer. She stumbled along the dock to stand right next to the giant sea creature.

Ben turned on a flashlight.

Amanda blinked at the brightness and let out an ungraceful squeak as the beam of light shone over a bare foot. The light traveled up the leg, torso, neck, to the face. She gasped as she recognized the body.

It was Robin McArthur.

TWENTY-FOUR

Setbacks

Complete darkness had settled in. The first responders had set up spotlights around the boat.

In the intense light, Chief Rodriguez's creased uniform was thrown into stark relief, and the adhesive bandage plastered over the slice on her cheek did little to conceal the tight set of her jaw.

"Would it do any good to tell her it's not my fault?" Amanda turned back to Detective Kim, who was taking her statement.

He shook his head. "Better just to leave her alone. Why don't you tell me what happened?"

"After we left you, we walked back to Ben's car so he could drive me home."

"From the accident in town? It was just as close to your sister's house as the marina. Why come here?"

"Ben thought I should eat. But when we arrived at his car, he didn't have his keys, so we came to his boat to get them, and there she was." As Amanda talked, she used her finger to trace their path from the parking lot through the docks, ending with both hands, palm up, pointing to the spot where the medical examiner's team was examining the body, minus Ben, who was standing with another officer on the far side of his boat. Realizing she looked like a game show host, she dropped her hands. "Is this my fault?"

"Why would you think that?" Detective Kim tilted his head.

"I told you and the chief that I thought Robin killed Tobias. And the next thing you know, she's dead. She was a victim, not the killer." Amanda shook her head. How could she have been so wrong?

"You're taking too much of this on yourself. You're not an investigator. It's true; you shouldn't be interfering. But my concern is more for your safety. Besides, you're correct; Robin didn't have an alibi. But we also haven't discovered a motive. She and Tobias worked together and got along well. Why would she have killed him?"

The detective was right. Amanda hadn't even considered motive. She had made another mistake, and like the one she made when she didn't follow her sister to California years ago, there were serious consequences.

The chief glared in their direction again.

Detective Kim straightened and looked down at his notes. "Well, thank you for the information." When the chief turned away, the detective whispered, "Right now, I'm a little more worried about Ben. He isn't taking this well."

Amanda was concerned, too. Not only was Robin dead on his boat, but the vessel had been ransacked. What wasn't water-soaked was now torn apart and dumped all over the damp carpet. There was no way Ben and Qbert could stay here tonight. Amanda wondered if he would ever be coming back to the boat.

Amanda hurried across the dock. "I'm so sorry, Ben."

"It's not your fault. What was Robin even doing on my boat?"

"Do you think she ransacked it? Silver said she had been searching boats. What could she have been looking for?" Amanda shivered in the cool night air.

They stood on the dock between Ben's and the Erlings' berths, watching the police process the scene. Across the marina, Jack waved his arms as he talked to Detective Kim, almost clipping one of Ben's staff as they moved in with a gurney.

Ben tensed, preparing to help, but then he sagged and shook his head. "I didn't have much of value here. Since the leak, I've stored most of my belongings in my office. All that's left here are some clothes, paperwork, and a few tools Mo left. Now that it's a crime scene, the police won't be letting her back on to finish the work anytime soon."

Amanda was about to invite Ben to stay with her and Qbert at her sister's house when a commotion at the gate caught everyone's attention.

Despite Silver's fears, Ocean Wood didn't have a paparazzi mill, but they did have two tenacious competing reporters. Both had somehow bypassed marina security and were now hurrying down the dock towards them, cameras up and snapping photos.

"Jack, as the marina manager, can you tell us what happened here?" Trevor Han of the *Tidepool Times* called out as an officer blocked his path.

"No comment, and this is private property; you need to leave," Jack hurried towards the intruders.

"Want to say anything to the public about the rash of murders that are occurring at your place of business?" Jill Bean of the *Ocean Wood Gazette* called out.

Jack blustered, "There hasn't been a rash. Just two!"

The woman smiled. "So, it was murder. Detective Kim, do you want to comment on how the police are addressing citizens' fears over this killing spree?" Jill Bean held her mini microphone up to the detective.

He shook his head and then motioned to one of the nearby officers to usher the reporters off the marina property.

After the newspaper reporters left, Detective Kim continued interviewing the people who had been around the marina that evening. Amanda could overhear what he was saying, but none of the information seemed to explain what had happened. And why were there so few people here? Amanda looked up at the enormous dark yacht beside them. Oddly, no one from the Erlings' vessel had come out to see what was happening.

"Ben, can I have a moment of your time?" The detective's tone was polite, but it wasn't a request that could be refused.

After the reporters left, Amanda stayed close to Ben for moral support. They were standing in the shadow of the powerful lights that had been set up around the boat. The man looked ready to cry as he watched the crime team blowing through his home leaving a trail of fingerprint powder in their wake.

"I'm sitting in on this interview." Chief Rodriguez's voice carried from the other side of the circle of lights, and the detective waited for the chief to join them.

Everyone inside the light pulled back and pretended not to watch, but they were listening.

"He already gave an official statement. I just have a few follow-up questions." The detective spoke in a slow, calming voice. "Ben, we can do this in the office if you want more privacy."

"No, I'd rather keep an eye on what they're doing."

"That's fine, as long as you stay here and don't try to board the boat. Can you tell me what happened before you arrived at the traffic accident this evening?"

"Amanda and I were on my boat talking. After she left, I decided to clean the kitchen, get it back to functional. I had just gotten started when Robin knocked. She said she'd heard that a pink van was in an accident outside the marina and did I know who that might be. I immediately thought of Amanda and grabbed my jacket and raced out. I don't think I even locked the door. By the time I got to the parking lot and realized I'd left my car keys on the boat, I could hear the sirens and I followed them up to where you all were."

"And you didn't see Robin get onto your boat?"

"No, but I didn't look back either."

"How did Robin seem?"

Ben took a second to think. "Strange. Stressed. I didn't think much of it at the time. She looked worried, and I probably just attributed that to having witnessed an accident. Come to think of it, she didn't say if she saw it or if someone else saw it and told her about it."

"How would that even be possible unless she or whoever saw it raced right here after it happened? You arrived almost as fast as the police did—" Amanda cut off speaking at the wide-eyed glare from the chief.

"So, just to confirm, the last you saw Robin alive, she was friendly, a little anxious, and outside your boat." The detective looked up from his notebook and witnessed Ben's nod.

"Okay, now let's talk about Tobias."

Ben stilled. "What about him?"

"Can you explain why his diving glove was found in your bedroom?"

Ben clenched his hands then released them. "I told you when Hartman found it, I have no idea how it got there."

"So, why did it have your fingerprint on the outside?"

Amanda stilled. What did that mean?

Ben was shaking his head, speechless.

The detective repeated his question.

Ben rubbed at his ear as if he couldn't believe what he was hearing. "How? I don't remember ever meeting Tobias, and to my knowledge I've never touched his or any diver's gear."

Amanda grabbed for his sleeve. "Ben, don't you need a lawyer before you say anything else?"

"But I didn't do this, and I don't know how that glove —" Ben broke off, stunned.

"Maybe we should finish this at the station," the detective offered again.

Ben's eyes narrowed. "Are you arresting me? Because I'd love to know what you came up with for motive."

"No. I just wanted to offer you some privacy."

"Well, I'm not going. And I have nothing more to say, so if you have any more questions, you can contact me through my lawyer." Ben squeezed Amanda's hand.

"Well, I have something to say." Chief Gina Rodriguez's face was bright red, and as she shook her head, her hair flew out of the unwinding bun. "We brought you in to help with the crime in this town, but you seem to be in the middle of it. You don't have an alibi for either murder. And it appears this one happened on your boat. You're already on administrative leave, and I can tell you that I'm seriously rethinking the city's arrangement to lease space to the medical examiner's office." She turned to the detective. "Get me answers by the end of the day tomorrow, or something more permanent will need to be done with him."

After the chief left, everyone working at the crime

scene was stunned. They continued their work in hushed tones, maneuvering around Ben like a piece of broken china.

Amanda didn't understand the delicate balance of politics that was going on, but she knew a threat when she heard one. Ben was in a lot of trouble.

TWENTY-FIVE

The Yacht

Soreness was beginning to set in, and Amanda really wanted to get home before she became too stiff. She headed over to Detective Kim to see if she was allowed to go. Just finishing up an interview, he thanked the couple who lived on a sailboat two slips down from Ben's, and as they left, he turned to Amanda.

"How are you doing?" He raised an eyebrow and pointed to the dock box behind him.

Amanda sat on the box and sighed. "Tired."

Detective Kim sat next to her. "When the adrenaline fades, that's all that's left."

"You were tough on Ben."

Detective Kim rubbed a hand over his face. "This is a murder inquiry. And that's why it's hard to make friends."

One of the Medical Examiner's Office team members broke from the group and headed towards them. The man in the full-length onesie did an awkward dismount from the boat and tripped over a light stand before he arrived, breathing hard. "You won't believe this. She was murdered too. Well, maybe. Possibly murdered. But guess what we found?"

Detective Kim tried to stop the man, but he was so excited he answered his own question.

"We found evidence that she was hit on the head." He paused. "And stabbed." His face lit up.

Amanda recognized the man. It was Andrew Meyers, the librarian's nephew.

"Can you believe it? I can't wait to get her back to the office."

Detective Kim frowned down at the younger man. "Thank you for the information, Andrew, but we try not to reveal any details of ongoing cases."

"Oh sure. That's why I waited until Ben was gone before I came over."

Detective Kim rubbed his thumb up the center of his forehead as he suppressed a grimace. "I'll look forward to the final report."

Andrew hitched up his pants beneath his onesie and took off at a trot to catch up with the rest of the team as they followed the gurney bumping along the dock.

"I'm sorry you heard that. Ben has been training him, but there's a way to go."

Amanda was too caught up in trying to understand what she had just heard. "Hit and stabbed...so, definitely murder, but which one killed her? And who would have a motive to kill both Robin and Tobias?"

"Amanda, I don't know why you want to get involved, but you need to leave figuring this out to the police."

"I'm trying to clear Ben's name."

"Sure… Your sister always had a really good reason why she was sticking her nose into investigations too, and now we don't know where she is."

Amanda didn't know what to make of that. Did the detective have information about her sister he hadn't told her?

Detective Kim continued, "And just a few hours ago, you found out someone tampered with your brakes. This case is way too dangerous for you to try out being an amateur sleuth."

"Okay, okay, but one more question. Don't you think it's odd that the Erlings aren't here? Have you talked to them?"

The detective looked up at the boat and shook his head. "Not really. They weren't suspects, as they've been staying in a hotel in town."

"Not every night." Amanda cocked her head at him and continued, "I know at least one night Mrs. Erling stayed here."

"Interesting. The husband and the mayor were together when the first death occurred. The wife was seen on camera entering and leaving the hotel several times. Maybe someone there can shed light on what happened that night and tonight."

The detective strode across the dock to the large yacht and, leaning in over the swim platform, called out, "Ocean Wood Police. Permission to come aboard?"

No response. After a minute, he tried again.

Amanda had followed the detective, ready to be sent

packing at any minute. When no one answered from the yacht, she followed up by knocking on the small door that she knew led to the crew quarters.

A minute later, the door cracked open.

The detective jerked in surprise when the skipper's booming voice asked, "Can I help you?"

"I'm Detective Kim of the Ocean Wood Police Department. I have a few questions about what happened here tonight. Can I come aboard?"

"Of course. Go up the steps, and I'll meet you at the first landing. Amanda can show you where." The skipper closed the door.

The detective turned to Amanda. "You can come on board, but you aren't sitting in on any questioning."

Amanda grinned and led the detective up to the main deck. The patio doors did not magically open this time, so they sat on the outside sun bed and waited.

A couple of minutes later, Jeffrey Cook joined them in a pressed white uniform, as if he were reporting for duty for the day. "How may I help you?"

The detective stood so he wasn't being towered over by the taller man. "Robin McArthur, the marina's sailing instructor... Can you tell me when you last saw her?"

"Blonde woman, right?" Jeffrey asked, and at the detective's nod, he added, "I've no need for sailing instructions, but I'm sure I've seen her around the marina."

The answer surprised Amanda. She had seen the skipper talking to Robin at least twice, and they acted like more than passing acquaintances.

"Is there anyone else on board this evening?" the detective asked, studying the skipper's face.

Captain Cook hesitated.

"Perhaps I should rephrase that. We would like to talk to whoever else is on board. Please bring them to us so we don't have to get a search warrant." Detective Kim returned to his seat on the sun lounger, indicating he planned to stay until that happened.

"Like the mayor would let you search this boat," the skipper scoffed, but he pulled out his phone and typed a quick message. Several minutes later, the patio door slid open. Captain Cook indicated they should go inside.

As the door closed behind them, Detective Kim frowned at Amanda, but he didn't ask her to leave.

With the custom lighting off, the interior was dark. The host, Mateo, emerged from the downstairs cabin area, his white uniform shirt wrinkled and untucked. He stepped aside and revealed the woman behind him.

A barefoot Mrs. Erling, with mussed hair and another silk robe, scowled as she flounced into the space. "What is this about?"

Detective Kim introduced himself again and repeated his question. "What can you tell me about Robin McArthur?"

"Who?"

"Robin McArthur, the marina's sailing instructor?"

"I've never taken a sailing class. How would I know him? Why have you woken me up to ask these questions?" More confident now, Mrs. Erling walked over to the couch and sat down in a huff.

Detective Kim pulled up a photo on his phone and showed it to Mrs. Erling. "Are you certain you don't know this woman?"

Mrs. Erling waved a dismissive hand.

The detective pocketed his phone. "Did you hear anything unusual this evening?" When no one spoke up, he added, "Any noises out of place for a boat or a marina? Any voices or shouting?"

"You mean like every civil servant in Ocean Wood clomping across the dock and banging on our boat?" Mrs. Erling's tone was scathing.

"This is an official police investigation, and if there is any doubt about your answers, I will require you to come to the station to discuss them."

"How dare you. My husband is friends with the mayor, and you bet he will hear about this."

"I'm asking reasonable questions to understand where you were when a crime occurred." Detective Kim smiled as he asked, "Can you confirm the three of you are here alone?"

Mrs. Erling's nostrils flared. "Yes, it's just us. No, I didn't hear anything. So, what happened to her?"

"Robin McArthur was found dead on the boat next to yours." The detective paused at Mrs. Erling's gasp of surprise. "It appears to be a suspicious death. I was told you all stayed at a hotel in town. Can you tell me why your plans changed and why you are here at the marina?"

"Well, it's very simple. I prefer sleeping on my yacht. We stayed in town the first night because the heater was broken, but the skipper fixed the problem, and now we're back."

"Without your husband," Detective Kim confirmed.

"Yes," Mrs. Erling snapped.

A whining sound came from the bottom of the stairs. Mateo hurried down the steps and returned with Poppy and Daisy. He put them down on the seat next to Luna. The minute they spotted the detective, they rushed to the edge of the cushion and growled. Then they saw Amanda. Tails wagging, they leaped from the couch and ran to her.

Amanda crouched down to greet them.

The detective returned to his questions. "And where were you two hours ago?"

"Why, we were here, eating dinner. Mateo created an amazing frittata. Is there anything else you need?"

Detective Kim shook his head. "That will be all for now." He put his notes in the pocket of his suit jacket.

"Then I suggest you schedule any future discussion through my husband's lawyers. Oh, and I'll be talking to the mayor about the dangerous lack of security here."

"Oh, you don't have to worry about that. We now have officers stationed at the gate and throughout the marina, checking anyone and anything coming and leaving."

Mrs. Erling sniffed and swept from the room with the flutter of silk. Poppy and Daisy each licked Amanda's hand then followed in a flounce.

TWENTY-SIX

Sneaking Around

"There's one more person you should talk to," Amanda told the detective as they stepped off the luxury yacht. "Officially, he doesn't live here."

Detective Kim tilted his head and studied her. "And unofficially?"

"He sees a lot of what goes on at the marina." Amanda walked off, hoping he would follow.

As they weaved their way through the docks to the opposite side of the marina, Amanda wondered aloud, "I thought this was a safe town. Now there are murders and break-ins. It's a little scary."

"It's a very safe town. These crimes are unusual and troubling."

"Has there been any news about the break-in at Alexandra's office?"

"I turned it over to the robbery division. They'll let me know if they find anything." Detective Kim nodded to an officer who let them pass into a darker section of the marina.

"You have a whole division?"

The detective hesitated then admitted, "We have a part-time guy, but he's very good."

Amanda sighed then shivered in the night air. "I feel like I'm being watched. It's creepy."

"Have you actually seen someone?" The detective's voice was concerned.

Amanda knew she didn't have more than glimpses of strange cars and intuition as proof. "No."

"Call the station if you see someone, and don't try to investigate this yourself. Your sister worked on dangerous cases."

Amanda agreed. She stopped beside a big silver-striped boat and knocked on the side. "Permission to come aboard?"

"Shhhh," a voice from inside hushed her. "Is anyone looking?"

"No," Amanda whispered back.

"Come on in," the deep voice replied.

Detective Kim raised an eyebrow at Amanda but followed her onto the dark boat. She headed up the steps and directly into the main cabin. As soon as the door closed behind them, a single light came on and surrounded the occupant in a pale white glow. The man lifted his head.

Detective Kim gasped. "You're Silver!"

The man laughed. His long, curly gray hair sparkled in the pale light. He was sitting on a large, curved sofa, dressed in jeans and a flashy shirt, and holding a tumbler of amber liquor.

"I'm a big fan. I didn't know you lived at the marina." The detective's hand trembled as he held it out to the rock star.

"Technically, he doesn't," Amanda clarified.

Silver sighed as he shook the offered hand. "Sorry about all the dramatics. The management won't give me liveaboard permission, something about liability and security, and my wife hasn't decided to let me return home yet. I'm not fond of hotels—too many decades touring—and the paparazzi always find me there. My boat is secure and comfortable." Silver indicated the detective's police badge hanging from his neck. "Are you here to arrest me?"

Recalling why they were there, Detective Kim pulled out his notebook. "I don't care that you're living here."

Silver smiled. "Well, you're all right. I knew Amanda wouldn't turn me in. Here, have a seat. What can I do for you?" Silver sat up from the sofa he'd been reclining on and patted the cushion beside him.

Amanda sat next to the aging rock star, turning so she could watch him while they talked. The detective chose to stay standing.

"I have to ask you a few questions about the body we just found."

"Another body?"

Amanda gave a silent, wide-eyed nod.

The detective ignored the singer's question and asked one of his own. "So, how long have you been living on your boat?"

"About two—no, three weeks. The missus and I got in a big fight. All my fault, of course. I've been sent here to think about my behavior." Silver's deep, gravelly voice was musical, and the cadence of his speech was like he was reading a poem.

"So, you were here this evening? You look dressed up. Did you go out?" Detective Kim pointed to the older man's outfit.

Silver plucked at his shirt. "This is how I always dress. I spent the last hour and a half on a virtual call with my agent. We're trying to coordinate the schedule for a new tour. Before that, I was on another call with the band. We're looking for a replacement for the local act that is supposed to open for the festival in a couple of weeks."

"Did you see or hear anything unusual during that time?"

"No, but bands are pretty loud. We recorded the call. I can ask my agent if we can give you a copy, as long as you promise not to leak the information to the paps." Silver reached into a mini fridge next to the sofa. "Can I offer you a drink? Beer? Water? Soda?"

Amanda asked for water, and he handed it to her. She unscrewed the lid and realized it was more than fatigue that was coming over her. The bruises from her accident were starting to make her body feel like she'd been tumbled dry. She wished she had a couple of painkillers she could take with the water.

Silver cocked an eyebrow at the detective, who shook his head. Closing the fridge, the singer refreshed his drink from a collection of bottles off to the side before he continued. "Something is going on in the marina. I've seen dark figures slinking around, staying in the shadows. And I caught Robin McArthur trying to break into my boat."

"When was that?" Detective Kim made a note in his book.

"About three days ago. I never asked her about it because I'd have to confess I was here." Silver leaned back and spread his arms over the back of the sofa.

The detective looked up from his notes. "What do you think Robin wanted?"

"I just assumed she was looking for something to sell. You wouldn't believe the strange things that turn up on the Internet that were supposedly mine; a half-eaten sandwich, the toilet seat from my childhood home... I caught my barber selling locks of my hair once." Silver chuckled.

Amanda nudged the singer's arm. "Tell him what happened two nights ago."

Detective Kim narrowed his eyes at her for taking over the interview.

"That's the night that boy was killed, wasn't it?" Silver asked Amanda. When she nodded, he turned to the detective and told him about spending the night drinking with Jack.

The detective raised a brow and wrote a note in his book. After a few more questions, he thanked the rock star and ended the interview.

Amanda left the boat with the detective, wincing as she jogged to keep up with the larger man's steps. It was dark out, but the recessed lighting on the storage boxes kept her from tripping.

"So, it's strange, isn't it, that everyone seems to have an alibi now except Robin? That's why I was sure she was the murderer. Murderess...? Is that a thing?"

The detective didn't comment.

"So, are we going to interview Mr. Erling now?" Amanda limped along beside him.

"*We* are not going to do anything. I realized when we were talking to Silver that the chief was right. You're like a kid with a stick poking at a hornet's nest. Someone has already tried to kill you today. And if you continue this way, they might succeed next time. So, I will see you safely back home, and then I expect you to keep your nose out of this investigation from now on." The heels of the detective's dress shoes tapped a sharp rhythm on the dock.

"Ben was going to drive me home." Amanda's shoulders slumped.

"You might not have noticed, but Ben has left."

Amanda glanced around the dark marina and realized the spotlights had been removed. Ben's boat was sealed off with crime scene tape, and everyone had left except for a few officers who looked like they were on patrol. "But my information was helpful, wasn't it?"

"This is a police investigation, and you need to stick to grooming dogs."

The detective drove Amanda back to her sister's house. She turned down his offer to check the property or escort her to the door, so he repeated his grim warning when she exited the car and then drove off.

Amanda sighed and turned to face the house. Today, she'd angered the chief again, she'd probably lost the

Erlings as clients, and Ben was mad at her. Detective Kim was warning her off. And now she had to go into the house and face Grok, who was already upset about the threat of the vet visit—and that was before he'd missed dinner.

Amanda tried to walk up the drive but instead turned around and headed across the street to Frank's house. At least there, she might get a sympathetic ear.

TWENTY-SEVEN

Refocusing

Frank answered the door in his customary clay-smeared polo shirt, khaki shorts, and rainbow-colored plastic shoes. "Woah... Who left puppy prints on your sunshine?"

Amanda tried to smile, but it came out a pout. "I think someone tried to kill me. Can we talk?"

Frank's mouth dropped open, and then he shook himself and stretched a protective arm over her shoulders as he glanced around. "Where? Are they following you? Have you called the police?"

"Yes, the police know. It happened earlier. Can we go to your studio?"

"Of course. Are we safe now?" Frank gave another wary look around the neighborhood.

Amanda nodded then followed Frank's gaze. "I think so."

Frank pulled the front door closed behind him, stopping to pop the lock. His long hair and big belly wobbled as he jogged to the garage door and punched in the code to raise the door. "Is this a cup of tea conversation, or do I need to break out the kombucha?"

Amanda shuddered. "Tea."

Frank, a former workaholic turned amateur potter, was the second person she had met in Ocean Wood, and they'd clicked almost immediately. She didn't know his husband well, but she had spent long hours talking with Frank in his garage studio.

Frank bypassed a bookcase of plywood and canvas shelves, where dozens of oddly shaped clay cups were drying, and headed for the counter set up with fixings for coffee and tea. He had converted the garage to a pottery studio, including a throwing wheel, canvas-covered tables, and drying racks. Water was added to a bright-orange electric kettle, and two mugs appeared, one with a bulging handle, the other with uneven sides. Frank added teabags then wiped down two chairs and set them on either side of a sturdy wood table.

"Milk? Sugar?"

"What type of tea?"

"Mocha mint."

"Milk, please."

Frank grunted in acknowledgment and put a kid-size carton of shelf-stable milk and a lumpy sugar bowl on a wooden board. He added bags to the mugs and filled them with boiling water. Then he brought the whole thing to the table and settled into one of the chairs. "While the tea steeps, why don't you tell me what's going on?"

Watching Frank go through the ritual of setting up the

tea had calmed Amanda's mind, but the anxious fear of messing up hadn't left. Still standing, she paced as she tried to put into words how she felt after everything that had happened that day. Finally, she settled on: "I'm disappointing everyone."

"Okay, why do you feel that way?"

Amanda threw up her hands.

"All I wanted to do was find the killer and clear Ben's name so he can stay here and get back to work, and instead, I'm causing him to run around town taking care of me. I told Detective Kim Robin was the killer, he warned me to stop investigating, and Robin ended up dead. And Chief Rodriguez was not happy that I crashed my RV into her squad car. I'm surprised she didn't kick me out of town."

Frank tried to cut in, but Amanda was on a roll.

She shoved a red curl that had dropped into her face behind her ear and added, "I came all this way to make up with my sister, and I don't know where she is. Did you know I found her casebook a couple weeks ago?" When Frank shook his head, she continued, "I don't know what it says. It's written in code, and I feel terrible that I've done nothing to try to find the cipher that breaks the code."

Amanda slumped into the chair with a groan and bowed her head.

"Wait, back up. What do you mean you had an accident? Are you okay? Was anyone hurt? Is that why you said someone tried to kill you?" Frank ran worried eyes up and down Amanda, settling on the hand she was holding to her side.

Amanda nodded. "Someone tampered with the Pink Pup's brakes, and I crashed into the chief's squad car. The chief got a scratch on her face, Detective Kim has a bruise on his chest from the steering wheel, and Grok left with all nine lives intact, but he's spitting mad at me. No one else was hurt."

"What about you? Do you even realize you're holding your side?"

"What? I'm not—" Amanda looked down and realized she had one hand clamped to her ribs. "Oh, that's just a pinch from the seat belt."

"Did you go to the hospital?"

"No, the EMTs checked me at the scene and said it was up to me. I don't have the money or the insurance to pay for a hospital visit. I'll put an icepack on the bruise when I get home."

Frank gave a reluctant head shake. "Why would someone try to kill you?"

"I don't know. Maybe I know something I don't know I know."

"You said Robin was dead? Are they sure it's suspicious?"

"Oh, it's very suspicious." Amanda explained what she had learned from Andrew.

Frank whistled. "It's obvious there's something going on at the marina, with first Tobias and now Robin dead. Why did you think that Robin killed Tobias?"

"She lied about her alibi, and I immediately jumped to the conclusion that it made her the killer, but what would have been her motive? She worked with Tobias and seemed to like him."

Amanda explained about meeting a "mystery man" who had seen Robin sneaking around and how suspicious it was that Luna Erling hadn't witnessed anything when it was happening right under her nose.

"Well, Ben didn't see anything, and it happened right under his boat." Frank sipped his tea. "Sounds like you're doing a better job at investigating than the police."

Amanda wasn't sure about that. "I just don't want Ben to leave."

"Besides an argument that he doesn't remember having and a pretty incriminating glove found on his boat, is there any motive for Ben to be involved with either death?"

"No," Amanda admitted.

"So, who would have a motive to kill both Tobias and Robin?"

"That's a very good question."

They talked more about repairs for the Pink Pup and an upcoming clay firing that Frank had scheduled for his work. Amanda left a little later feeling calmer and resolved to put everything aside for the night—except for dealing with Grok—and look at the murders with fresh eyes in the morning.

TWENTY-EIGHT

The Maple Syrup Incident

Early the following day, Amanda received an emergency call from Mrs. Erling. Poppy had been involved in a maple syrup incident and needed an immediate bath. Thinking of the van and how much it would cost to fix, she quickly accepted the job and hauled her aching body out of bed.

To her surprise, Mrs. Erling provided an address for the hotel in town. The short walk helped ease Amanda's stiffness. She entered the hotel through the service entrance at the back and followed the directions to the front desk. They escorted her to the top floor, where Mateo ushered her into a large suite.

"Oh, thank goodness you're here." Mrs. Erling frowned as she clipped on a pearl earring. She wore pristine cream pants and a delicate, layered silk blouse that flowed as she walked. "It's a disaster."

Turning her back, she shrugged into a tailored cream jacket and spoke over her shoulder. "Alan ordered pancakes for breakfast. We looked away for a minute, and Poppy was on the table, eating them and dragging her coat through all that maple syrup. She's a mess. Mateo put her in the bathtub."

"Poor thing. Can I wash her here? I would take her to the grooming RV, but yesterday—"

Mrs. Erling waved a dismissive hand. "Yes, yes, whatever. Talk to Mateo. He can get you whatever you need. We're heading out to a meeting with the mayor. Come, baby."

Daisy rushed into the room as fast as her legs would carry her, her silky hair flowing around her. The woman in white scooped her up and air kissed her then handed the little Pekingese to Amanda and picked up a pair of gold cuffs from the coffee table, snapping them onto her wrist before calling out into the suite of rooms, "Darling, we're going to be late."

A tall, gray-haired man strutted out of the back room. "You must be the groomer I've heard so much about." He held out a hand for Amanda and gave her a wide politician's grin. "Thank you for helping us out this morning."

"Have you been in town long?" Amanda asked, returning the handshake.

"We've been here a few days. It's nice to catch up with old friends, and Mother loves to see us." Alan Erling put on a sports jacket that matched his open-collared shirt.

"I was surprised you stayed in a hotel instead of your beautiful boat," Amanda pushed, hoping the man would continue to talk.

"We've been having trouble with the heater on the

yacht, so we've been slumming it here instead." Mr. Erling waved around the luxuriously gold and beige-styled room. Then he straightened his cuff over an expensive-looking watch that gleamed with diamonds.

"That's a beautiful watch."

"Thank you. It's new." He turned towards Mrs. Erling. "Ready, darling?"

"Why don't you head downstairs, dear? I'll just be a moment." Mrs. Erling smiled at her husband.

As soon as the door closed behind him, she turned on Amanda, the smile gone. "I want to make sure there are no misunderstandings about what you saw last night."

Amanda realized this was about more than just Poppy's coat.

"My husband is a very important man and doesn't have time to waste on unfounded rumors or suppositions. I expect if you have any questions, you will come to me with them. Is that a problem?" Mrs. Erling crossed her arms, her bracelets making clinking sounds like ice in a glass.

"No problem at all." Amanda's checks heated as she agreed. "So, does Poppy still need a bath?"

"Of course. She's covered in syrup. I will pay you double for your rush. I'm glad we have an understanding." Mrs. Erling picked up a cashmere throw and wrapped it around her shoulders, leaving Amanda in a cloud of perfume.

"You ready?" Mateo asked.

"Is it that bad?" She checked Mateo out for the first time and saw the amber stains on his dress shirt and pants.

"It's a good thing we have a great dry cleaner. They can get out anything but blood. I had to chase her all over the room. We've got housekeeping coming to change the bedding and steam the carpets while they're gone." Mateo walked deeper into the suite, and Amanda could see the trail as if a broom had swept the sticky syrup until it faded out.

Mateo pulled Daisy from Amanda's arms as he opened the door, gave Amanda a little shove through, and closed the door behind her, calling out, "Good luck."

Excited yip-yaps greeted Amanda as Poppy tried to climb the sides of the enormous tub. She was covered in syrup with bits of pancakes and other debris stuck to the sticky mess. How did she get it on her ears?

For a minute, Amanda wondered if Luna had poured the syrup over the dog so she would have an excuse to call her and warn her off saying anything. Then she realized what a ridiculous idea that was.

Whatever the reason, Poppy needed her help. She shrugged out of her grooming backpack and pulled out an apron. Then she pulled out the other tools she would need and put a towel on the floor for her knees.

Poppy made a whimpering sound and butted her head into Amanda's hand when she reached in to pet her.

Turning to the little Pekingese, Amanda reassured her. "Don't worry, love. We'll get you cleaned and playing with Daisy again soon."

TWENTY-NINE

A New Bed to Lie In

Best Friends Boutique turned out to be a lifesaver once again. Since Amanda moved to Ocean Wood, the shop owner, Katrina, regularly entrusted her with grooming her two dogs and frequently referred clients her way.

Amanda called the shop as soon as she left the hotel.

Katrina was thrilled to hear she was available. "My regular groomer blew a gasket yesterday when a client was late for an appointment. She had a total meltdown, stormed out, and didn't return. I hate to admit it, but I was relieved to see her go. You're welcome to work with your clients. I just need someone to cover the shop some-times and take walk-in grooming projects. When can you start?"

"I can be there in fifteen minutes." Amanda started to jog.

Katrina laughed. "I'll see you when you get here, and you don't have to run."

Amanda slowed to a walk, panting into the phone as she ended the call.

The rest of her afternoon went surprisingly smoothly as she transitioned her clients from mobile appointments to a drop-off at the boutique.

Amanda was covering the shop while Katrina went to lunch when Grok turned up demanding food. She had no idea how he found her, and she wondered for a minute if he had put a tracker on her before she remembered his nose *was* the tracker.

"How long are we going to be working here? I'm bored." The big cat swung a lazy paw at a cat teaser stick with a rubber mouse dangling on the end. The pink mouse got stuck in his claw. Grok rolled away, pulling his arm back, then let go. The pink mouse shot across the room, taking out a row of stuffed dogs lining the front counter. Grok snickered.

"Knock that off! We're here until I can make enough to get the Pink Pup fixed." She picked up the half dozen stuffed dogs scattered around the floor and lined them back up by the register. Then she took a cat backpack off the shelf with the dog toys and moved it back to the correct rack.

Grok wandered the room and pounced on a giant dog bed, walking the four corners as if trying it on for size. "If we'll be coming here from now on, I'll need this."

"Fine, but you have to keep it out here and behave. I don't want it getting wet in the back, and for some unfathomable reason, the customers like you."

"Of course they do. I'm adorable," Grok declared as he

pulled the new bed over to a spot in the window that caught the best sun. By the end of the day, Grok had sold three of those beds.

Amanda was wrapping up her last client when the bell rang. Katrina had already left for the day and had given her a key to lock up. When Amanda came out of the back room, she was surprised to see a short, broad man wearing an expensive suit sorting through a rack of doggy tutus. She had only met him once since moving to Ocean Wood. "Mayor Shore? Welcome to Best Friends Boutique. Can I help you find something?"

As the mayor turned away from the rack of costumes, a sparkle caught Amanda's eye. Expecting it to be a misplaced sequin from a tutu, she glanced down at the mayor's wrist in time to see him tug a cuff over an expensive-looking watch, the face circled by diamonds.

"I'm not here to buy. I'm here to see you, Amanda. I'll get right to the point. I understand you have been misrepresenting yourself as part of an open police investigation. I received complaints that you've been questioning the Erlings, disrupting their visit to Ocean Wood." The mayor's tone was severe, but his face continued to carry the jovial expression of a seasoned politician. He paused for effect and then carried on. "Alan Erling's mother is one of Ocean Wood's most distinguished residents. Do you know she is considering a donation to update Butterfly Grove Park? Millions of dollars that will benefit the citizens of Ocean Wood, put in jeopardy by your interference in a police investigation." The mayor stopped, but not long enough for Amanda to respond before he continued. "Do you feel Chief Rodriguez can't handle this?"

As if sensing her distress, Grok jumped from his bed and stood with her, wrapping his tail around one of Amanda's ankles.

"I was just talking to them. They're a client. I didn't mean to misrepresent myself to them," Amanda stammered. "I certainly didn't imply that anyone at the police station had approved—"

The mayor shook his head. "Let me be blunt. Don't talk to the Erlings. Allow the police to conduct the investigations. Understood?" The mayor finished in a tone that implied an answer was not required, and he turned to leave.

Amanda knew she was already in trouble, so she might as well put that final nail in the coffin. "Your watch is gorgeous. Where did you get it?"

The mayor stopped. Amanda assumed he would show off the watch. Instead, he lowered his cuff to cover his wrist. "It was a gift from my daughter."

"It looks expensive."

"It's a knockoff. I may be a humble civil servant, but I have to keep up appearances with wealthy donors." Narrowing his eyes, he took a step towards her. "It's interesting to see you have some of the same characteristics as your sister. Flittering around like our famous butterflies, sticking your noses where they don't belong. You need to understand how things are done in this town. Keep out of police investigations if you don't want to end up sharing her fate."

A sudden chill washed over Amanda. Did the mayor of Ocean Wood just threaten her? Did the man know something about her sister's disappearance?

Falling back, Amanda struggled to retain her footing and find her voice. "What—"

Before she could finish, the mayor left the shop.

Amanda sagged against the front desk, unsure what to make of the encounter. "What just happened?"

Grok jogged to the front of the store. Getting up on his hind legs, he put his front paws on the door and glanced down the street to ensure the mayor had indeed left. "I don't know."

"That was weird, right?" Amanda asked him.

Grok made a rumbling hiss of agreement as he paced like a mountain lion in front of the shop's windows. He turned his big head towards her. "Something is not right in this town."

THIRTY

Messing Up

Amanda's spirits were low as she walked back to her sister's house at day's end. She chose the shoreline route home, hoping to lift her mood. But even with the sun's warmth lingering on the sand and the waves gently lapping the rocks, her gloom persisted. Being threatened by Mayor Shore felt like the ultimate sign that Amanda wasn't welcome in Ocean Wood. Ever since she had arrived looking for her sister, she had let down one person after another. After her conversation with Frank, she realized Chief Rodriguez would never be her fan. But now the mayor said her interference could cost the town a considerable donation. And Ben was still thinking about leaving town.

"I've completely messed up, Grok." Amanda waved her hands in the air as she spoke.

"What do you mean?" Grok was striding alongside her.

"I mean, I failed. I'm trying to find out who killed

Tobias so I can clear Ben's name and he won't leave. Instead, I've just made everyone angry." Her hands dropped to her sides, and her shoulders sagged.

Grok laughed wickedly. "Oh, that's not failure. The angrier they get, the more you stir them up, the more you know you're heading in the right direction. You'll know you're about to find the killer when someone starts taking shots at you."

"You're kidding, right? Don't you think tampering with the RV's brakes was enough?" Amanda glanced over at Grok.

"When I ran investigations, everybody hated me, and I had the highest success rate in the space force," Grok said, not missing a beat as he followed beside her.

Amanda stopped in the middle of the sidewalk. Dropping her purse to the ground, she gentle knelt and reached a hand out to the cat.

"How do you feel right now?" Her voice was soft. Amanda was trying not to startle Grok, unsure if he knew what he'd said. In that one statement, he'd revealed more about his past than he had ever said before, and he hadn't gone into a seizure and blacked out.

"What do you mean?" Grok asked.

Amanda switched tactics. "How long were you with the space force? And what was your rank?"

"I was there for five of your Earth years and was the lead investigator—" Grok's voice trailed off. His face scrunched up as he let out a yowl of pain and dropped to his belly. He covered his ears with both paws as his whole body shook.

Amanda scooted forward, careful not to touch him. She knelt beside him, watching over the cat until the seizure passed and Grok's yowls diminished to soft pants.

"Are you okay?" Amanda used the softest, quietest voice she could.

Grok clamped his paws tighter over his ears.

She settled cross-legged beside the cat and waited. They were in the grass at the end of the sidewalk. Cars passed, slowing through the residential neighborhood. Amanda noted the automatic lights popping on in the houses around them as it grew dark.

Grok groaned.

She turned her attention back to the cat.

He lifted his head, gently swinging it around. "Where am I? Why are you sitting on the ground? Owww..." The cat's eyes closed, and he dropped his head again.

Amanda gave him a minute before whispering, "Are you okay now? You had another seizure. I'm so sorry. I pushed you and asked questions I shouldn't have. Do you remember anything?"

Grok started to shake his head then thought better of it; his voice was raspy. "You were whining about being a failure, and then I felt blinding pain. Did I say something brilliant and solve the problem?" He lifted his head and blinked.

Amanda got up. Grok was feeling better if he was snarking again. "Sure. What you said made all the difference."

"Do you think you can walk?" Amanda indicated the

turn up ahead that veered away from the ocean and headed towards the house.

Grok gave a grunt of acknowledgment, and Amanda started walking, turning back to check if Grok was coming. The cat hopped up and followed her, weaving a little.

When Grok caught up with Amanda, they walked in silence for several minutes.

"Feeling better?"

"Feeling the need for a distraction." The cat sneezed as a car turned a corner and spun up a mini dust cloud. "So, what do we know?"

Amanda guessed that they weren't going to talk about the amnesia so she quipped, "You mean about the murder? Or about my potentially being driven out of town?"

"You worry too much about what other people think. Who cares? Humans are bad character judges anyway." Grok stumbled beside her. His stride lacked its normal stealthiness, but Amanda chose not to say anything or ask if he needed help.

"I would roll my eyes at you, but that's a pointless human behavior, so I shall not." Amanda turned up her nose at Grok.

"Listen, it helps to go over it. Now, what do we know about the original murder?"

They turned down Lily Street, and Amanda started to search for the keys in her purse. With her head in her bag, she responded, "We know Tobias died just before midnight two nights ago. We know a spear gun killed him and we know there have been break-ins at the marina but we don't know if the thefts are related." Amanda jiggled the keys in her hand, tilting her head to the side as she thought. "We don't know much."

"Didn't you say people were seen arguing with him earlier that day? Both Jack and Ben?"

"Hey, the point is to clear Ben's name."

"The point is to find the killer and not be a sentimental—"

"Human," Amanda finished for him as she reached to unlock the door and paused. A cold trickle of awareness ran down her back. *Were they being watched again, or was she always going to feel paranoid?*

Glancing over her shoulder, she scanned the street. That strange man had been following her. It wasn't unreasonable to think he was out there watching her now.

Oblivious to her mood, Grok paced the porch. "No, we don't have a lot of information. But we do know people who could find out more."

"Who?"

"Those weirdos you call friends."

"Hey, they aren't weird! And they're your friends too —who fed you when Alexandra went out of town?"

Grok shrugged.

"They did!"

"Fine, they're eccentric but reliable," Grok conceded with an unhappy hiss.

"But that's a good idea. We could invite Frank, Dot, and Albert over after dinner to see if they can help us." Amanda opened the lock and rushed through the door, wishing Grok would hurry up and follow.

"That's a good plan, as long as it doesn't make dinner

late. Now, I thought the salmon chowder you made a few weeks ago would be perfect for tonight. Chop, chop. You must cook fast so we can start the sleuthing." Grok pushed into the house.

Amanda shook her head. Was it a mistake not to tell Grok what he'd said before the seizure? Based on his physical reaction whenever faced with a memory, she didn't think it was. She would add this to the journal she kept on the cat. Maybe someday, all these pieces of information would make sense.

THIRTY-ONE

Start at the Beginning

While Amanda made the salmon chowder for dinner, she tried to work up her nerve to ask for help. They were her friends. Well, they'd been very friendly to her since she arrived—when she wasn't suspecting them of murder. Having people who came when you called for help was a new concept for her. Finally, as Grok finished his first bowl of soup, Amanda fished her phone out of her pocket and made the call.

While she waited for someone to answer, she looked out over the backyard and wondered what her sister would think of her taking over her house. Would she have been welcomed?

"Hello? Amanda?"

"Dottie, I could use some advice."

Dottie was thrilled to be involved in the investigation. She promised to let the others know and said they would be there in an hour with wine.

Amanda finished eating, tidied the kitchen and the

living room, and then thought about what they might need. Remembering the whiteboard on an easel in the kitchen, she moved both items into the living room and was hunting for markers when she heard people talking outside.

She opened the front door and found Albert with bottles of wine tucked on either side of him in his chair, and Dot was carrying a box of glasses. "We weren't sure how stocked your house was."

"Alexandra doesn't have much kitchenware, so it's a good thing you brought resources. Albert, do you know where the ramp is in the back? I'll meet you there." After he nodded, Amanda moved to shut the door. There was a call from the street.

"Hold up." Frank was slowly walking up the gravel drive in his rainbow-colored rubber shoes, holding a wooden charcuterie board. Amanda held the door open for him. "Sorry Bob couldn't make it, but I brought cheese!"

"That looks lovely. We're going to set up here in the living room. Make yourself comfortable while I grab the door for Albert and Dottie," Amanda hurried to the back door.

As everyone settled, she realized she needed something for notes. Amanda unlocked the drawer on her sister's desk. She eyed her sister's casebook with a pang of frustration then pushed it aside. Underneath were several packs of sticky notes and colored whiteboard markers. She grabbed what she needed and locked the drawer again.

Clearing her throat, Amanda stuttered while her nerves settled. "Th-Thanks for coming. I could really use your help. I'm not making a lot of progress on finding Tobias's killer and clearing Ben's name. I had a visit from the mayor today, and he warned me to keep my nose out of this, or else..."

"Or else what? What did that little worm say to you?" Frank jumped up from where he had settled on the over-stuffed couch.

"The Erlings must have complained that I was asking them questions, and they threatened to pull a donation to the city if I didn't stop. He..." Pulling at her collar, Amanda cleared her throat. "He implied I was going to end up like Alexandra. Do you think he knows what happened to her?"

"He said what?" Frank pulled his phone from his back pocket and was tapping away. "I'm going to call him right now."

"Oh, no, please don't." Amanda was sure that would make things worse.

"You can't," Albert insisted. "You'll tip him off. You need to find out first if he knows something about these deaths and Alexandra's disappearance."

A horrible thought occurred to Amanda. "You don't think they're related, do you?"

"Why would they be? Little Rocky's just trying to be a big shot and push people around. He's always been like that. You should have seen the little snot when he was in high school." Dottie made a sound of disgust.

Frankly, Amanda thought he was more upsetting now

than he could have been as a teenager, but she didn't tell Dottie that.

"Fine." Frank's face was red, and a muscle ticked in his jaw as he sat back down.

"So, excluding the mayor, where should we start?" Amanda tapped a marker against her chin.

Grok padded into the room, weaving among the chairs, and leaped onto the couch. He slid across the back until he covered half the surface and lay on his side. "You should start with the victim."

"We should start with the victim," Amanda repeated, trying not to look at Grok. With a red marker, she wrote Tobias's name at the top of the board. Now what?

"Don't forget the other human," Grok added, starting to groom his front paw as if he had just discovered it.

"That's right," Amanda replied to the cat.

The others looked puzzled.

"Sorry, I just remembered that we have to add Robin's name."

After adding the woman's name in a separate column, she listed under each name how they died and the suspected time of death.

"Are you serious? She was stabbed and bludgeoned?" Dottie acted out each action, ending with a collapse onto Albert's lap. "Which one killed her?"

"They don't know yet, but as you can imagine, they've ruled out accidental death." Amanda ignored the loud snort from Grok.

"So, you thought Robin killed Tobias, but then she ended up dead?" Frank crossed his arms.

"Yes. I have no idea what her motive would have been. She mentioned they worked together but weren't close, but you should have seen her... She looked utterly devastated when she found out he was dead." Amanda remembered how the tan sailing instructor's face turned ghostly pale at the news.

"Do we know if anyone might have had a grudge against Tobias?" Albert swiveled his chair to face the whiteboard. Dottie, still sitting in his lap, raised her foot to swing it over the coffee table where the food was laid out.

"Ms. Meyers in the library told me a very interesting story about Tobias. He has a reputation for finding rare items."

"She would know," Frank muttered. At Amanda's cocked head, he added, "Our librarian is multifaceted. Don't let the sweater sets fool you. But never mind that. Most people didn't know about Tobias's business. That is something we should learn more about."

Amanda started a list of questions. "I know Jack was seen arguing with him. And he's the one who said there was a break-in, so whoever the thieves were are strong suspects."

"How did they get in? The marina is locked up at night." Frank bit into a cracker, swiping at the flakes that landed down the front of his shirt.

Amanda added that to her list of questions.

"Who else had access?" Dottie jumped up and started pacing.

"Well, there's Jack, Luna, Mateo, the skipper, and

Silver." Amanda wrote down each name. "At least, those are the people who were at the marina that night."

"Silver, the Rockstar? I love him and his band, Electric Sandwich. Did you meet him? Did he say he's performing at the upcoming Butterfly Music and Art Festival?" Frank jumped up and pulled his phone from his pocket again. "We should have his music going on while we do this. It'll be our theme song."

Albert raised a brow at Frank. "I love Silver's music too, but it's not exactly conducive to deductive reasoning."

"Oh, what do a detective and a guitarist have in common?" Dot paused for dramatic effect before saying, "They both pluck at strings." She fell forward, laughing, while the rest of us groaned.

"Amanda, I hate to tell you this, but you forgot the most obvious suspect." Frank walked over and picked up one of the markers. He added Ben's name to the list in capital letters. "You said Robin saw him and Tobias getting into it, he had the best access, and they found that glove..."

As if summoned, there was a knock at the door.

THIRTY-TWO

A Plan

When Amanda answered the front door, she found Ben, shoulders slumped, on the porch with Qbert on a leash beside him. The dog wagged his tail in welcome. "Amanda, I need a favor." His voice was flat.

"Of course. Come on in." She grabbed Ben's arm and pulled him inside, where he was greeted with a chorus of welcomes.

"How's the boating life?" Albert asked, turning his chair towards the door.

"You know the boat sprung a leak, but now I've found out its gotta be pulled from the water for repairs. Which can't be done until it's cleared as a crime scene." A pained expression crossed Ben's face, and he blew out a breath. "I'm here to beg for a place to stay. I tried crashing at the office, but it was impossible to get any sleep."

"Of course. You're always welcome here. Have you eaten?" Amanda herded Ben deeper into the living room. The others fussed over him while she took Qbert into the kitchen. She left the dog happily munching on a plate of Grok's high-end cat food and took a bowl of chowder to Ben.

Ben settled on the couch with a groan. Then he caught sight of the suspect board. "What were you doing before I got here?"

Dot jumped up from her seat and rushed to place her 4'7" frame in front of Ben's name on the board. "Nothing's happening here. We were just playing charades," she said, making wild gestures.

"It's a loon!" Albert called out.

Dottie frowned at her husband.

"Looks like you were trying to solve a murder." Ben took a spoonful of soup. His eyes widened, and he stared into the bowl and took a second bite.

"I can explain..." Amanda stepped in front of the board next to Dot and tried to figure out what to say.

Frank cleared his throat. "Amanda thought if she solved the crime, she could save your job and you would stay in town. We were just lending a hand."

"Well, what do you have? Maybe I can help." Ben tilted his head to see the board around them.

"Really?"

"Amanda, don't look so surprised. I'm as eager to get this one figured out as you." Ben pointed to his name on the board. "And just so you know, I don't remember meeting Tobias and I have no idea how that glove got on my boat."

There was an awkward silence after Ben's statement.

"Well, we should find out more." Amanda added questions about the argument and glove to the list. Relieved Ben wasn't mad, she then explained to him what they knew.

"Jack, the marina manager, said there were thefts, but were they ever reported? And Robin told me that Jack was fighting with Tobias. But Robin also told me that she was with Jack when Tobias was killed. Silver also claimed Jack was with him." Amanda searched her mind. Was there anything she had missed?

"And we know that Jack was taking bribes," Ben added.

"What about those people on the yacht? What's their motivation?" Dot asked.

"Alan Erling's mother is a big deal in Ocean Wood. And Alan is tight with the mayor. It would have to be something pretty big if they were involved." Frank crossed his arms as he sat back on the sofa next to Ben.

"Like an affair?" Amanda asked.

"An affair between the mayor and Alan?" Dot's eyes grew huge.

Frank choked back a laugh. "Not likely."

"No, an affair between Mrs. Erling and a crew member. I don't exactly know his job; his name is Mateo." Amanda explained the conversation that she and Detective Kim had with Mrs. Erling earlier that day.

"But if Luna is having an affair, why would she kill Tobias or Robin?" Albert asked, always the voice of reason in their group.

Ben finished chewing and wiped his mouth. "Maybe

they saw something. Nothing is private at the marina. If Luna and Alan broke up, big money would be involved."

"They also have alibis if they all stayed at the hotel that night. But I don't know how to confirm that," Amanda said.

"I hate to state the obvious…" Grok's voice was bored, and he didn't bother lifting his head from the back of the sofa. "But our first step should be checking all of the alibis. Some of them are weak. You also need to look deeper at motives. Nothing so far sounds like a real motive for murder."

Amanda tried hard not to glance at Grok as he spoke.

"Amanda, are you okay?" Ben looked where she was staring and saw Grok. He gave the cat a friendly pat.

"I was just thinking nobody has a good motive for either of the murders," Amanda said as she thumped the marker against her chin.

"Well, I'm going to talk with Rocky and find out more about the Erlings and their alibi. And I'm going to talk to him about how he treated you. That kind of bullying isn't acceptable." Frank put on his ruthless businessman face.

"I can find out what information they have on Robin's death. I have a great alibi since I was with Amanda, Gina, and Adam," Ben volunteered.

Amanda frowned at Ben. "I know Gina is Chief Rodriguez, but who is Adam?"

"Detective Adam Kim." Ben smiled as Amanda's mouth dropped open.

"Guess I didn't catch his first name when he was questioning me." Amanda scowled.

Dot grabbed Albert's hand. "What if we find out more about spearfishing in this area? Albert can do some research online. I can check with a buddy at the raceway, see if there is anything special about thefts occurring in the area lately."

Amanda frowned. "Don't put yourself in danger."

"I won't. This guy is well connected, but he'll tell me upfront if I need to keep my nose out of something."

Amanda put down the marker. "Well, that leaves learning more about Tobias and the marina for me. I'll head back tomorrow to see what I can discover about his employment there and how the place works. Maybe I can find someone besides the skipper who knows why Jack and Tobias were arguing."

With a plan in place, a sense of excitement went through Amanda, and for the first time, she felt like she could actually make a difference.

The conversation changed to local events in Ocean Wood, including the upcoming music festival and Amanda's encounter with the famous musician Silver.

When Albert grew tired, he and Dot said their goodnights, and Frank followed soon afterward.

"I hope you don't mind staying in Alexandra's room." Amanda led Ben down the hall to her sister's bedroom.

"At this point, I could sleep on a rock as long as it was dry." Ben's chuckle sounded like a sigh.

Amanda grabbed fresh sheets and towels from the linen closet and motioned down the hall to the door at the end.

Ben entered the room and stood at the threshold. That

was as far as Amanda had gotten in the past, and she felt strange about invading her sister's privacy, but she pushed past him and started to pull the blankets and sheets off the bed. The room was tidy and organized, as Amanda would have expected from her sister. Which is what made the state of her office so confusing. She didn't know Alexandra anymore, but from everything she had learned, her sister would have been the first to offer someone in need a place to stay.

"I can do that," Ben said even as he sank into a comfortable chair in the corner of the room.

"Don't bother. You look dead on your feet. Why don't you get Qbert set up?" She tossed a set of flannel sheets to Ben.

He made a comfortable pallet on the floor next to the window that the dog immediately settled into. When Amanda was done, he sank face-first onto the bed, toeing off his shoes before he grabbed a pillow.

"Goodnight," Amanda whispered, pulling the door closed but leaving it open enough for Qbert to get out.

Amanda was still too excited by all her friends' support to sleep. She curled up on the couch with her sister's casebook and shared a pile of fluffy blankets with Grok. After a half hour of staring at the same page with no idea how to break the code, she realized she was done for the night.

While she was locking up the house, Grok cornered her in the kitchen, a scowl twitching his whiskers. "Why did everyone get an assignment but me?"

"I was worried after your blackout earlier that you might not feel up to helping."

"I'm fine to assist the investigation, if it's a task worthy of my skills."

Amanda smirked. One issue had been pressing on her mind. Grok was the perfect candidate, but she didn't want the cat to think he was doing busy work. "Well, this isn't about the murders, but you're the perfect cat for the job. We need to find out who the bald man in black is. There's more to it than him searching for Alexandra, and I don't know how, but we need to find out what he knows."

Grok sat back on his haunches and tilted his head. His whiskers wiggled. "You're right. I sense the same thing. This is a task worthy of my attention."

Amanda tried not to laugh at Grok's modesty. "Excellent. The sooner we learn what he knows, the faster we find Alexandra. While you look into that, I'll head back to the marina first thing in the morning to talk to the staff and check out the scene again. There's got to be something about Ben's boat that both bodies were found so close to it."

Grok nodded his approval and padded toward his automatic cat door.

"Are you going out now?"

Grok looked back at her, his tail twitching. "The night is for hunting."

THIRTY-THREE

The Key

The following morning, Grok still hadn't returned from hunting.

"I've got a meeting. Do you want me to drop you at the marina?" Ben adjusted the black glasses sliding down his nose. He was dressed for work in navy pants and a dress shirt buttoned to his throat.

Amanda reached out a hand and flicked the top button open.

Ben's eyes bulged. He turned to look in the mirror by the door. "Isn't that kind of daring?"

"Technically you're on leave. Oh, hang on a second. I need to find you a key."

Amanda rummaged in the bowl by the door where she had initially found the key she was using. Hers had a string and a paper tag labeled "spare" attached.

Holding up each key, she compared them to hers. "None of these match."

"What about that?" Ben pointed to a key chain with

several keys and a short metal bookmark engraved with random letters.

"I think those are Alexandra's keys." Amanda held back from touching them.

"Why are they here? Wouldn't they be with her?"

Amanda was stunned. He was right. This was another thing to add to her list of clues from Alexandra's disappearance.

Ben picked up the keys and tried each in the front door. "This one works. I'll keep it and the key ring, and you can take the rest of these." Ben separated the keys.

As Amanda took a deep breath and accepted the keys, her stomach tightened. She knew she couldn't memorialize every item of her sister's, but a key ring was personal. It was carried everywhere you went and spent so much time in your hand. Discomfort warred with the practical. One of those keys undoubtedly opened the PI office, and she would have known if she had been using them all along.

"Come on." Ben put a comforting hand on her shoulder then headed out the door.

Amanda followed, leaving the shadow of doubt behind.

Ben dropped her and Qbert off at the marina. Her first client wasn't until late morning, so she had time to snoop around. She wanted to see Ben's boat, the scene of the second murder, in the light.

Luck was on her side when she caught the front gate as someone was leaving. On her way to Ben's boat, she ran across the aging rockstar also sneaking into the marina.

"Good evening!" Silver's enthusiastic wave unbalanced

him. He weaved on the dock, almost knocking his sunglasses off, before steadying himself.

"Don't you mean good morning?" Amanda looked up at the bright-blue sky.

"I haven't been to bed yet. It was a glorious night. Those politicians know how to party." Silver threw his arms wide. "What brings you to the slumbering sails? Oh, that is good. I should write it down—I've got a piece of paper here somewhere." He pulled a pair of purple lacy panties out of his pocket. "Now I just need a pen." He patted his other pockets.

Amanda chewed on her lip. "Can I ask you another question?"

Silver abandoned his task and turned towards her, over-spinning and wobbling as he stepped back and nodded for her to follow him. "I'm an open book—nothing to hide, clear as crystal. I call a spade a spade. Let's lay all of our cards on the table and let the cat out of the bag," Silver proclaimed loudly, obviously forgetting he was trying to sneak in.

"Is that one of your songs?" Amanda followed Silver onto his boat and up the back stairs. She tied Qbert to one of the hitches, and he spread out in the shade of the sun bed.

Silver grabbed his chest as if struck with a knife. "You kill me. You've never heard that song before? It was number one for six weeks—a few decades ago." Silver's face lit up as he intently stared at his thumb as he tried to snap his fingers. "That's sooooo hard! Never mind. S-N-A-P." He spelled out the word. "Here is what we'll do. I'll get you tickets to the upcoming festival, and you can hear me perform it live, 'kay?" Silver unlocked the patio doors to his cabin and slid them open. Stumbling over the threshold, he collapsed onto the sofa and waved her towards a chair.

Amanda declined the seat offer and got down to business. "You said you were with the office manager, Jack Roberts, when Tobias was killed. Was that true?"

"Yes..." Silver paused long enough for Amanda to start her next question, and then he continued speaking. "And no." He wiggled his eyebrows at her.

"What do you mean?" Amanda sank into the chair.

"I mean, I was with Jack that night. We did a lot of drinking. I couldn't tell you who was or wasn't on the boat after I fell asleep—or passed out. I must have gotten up, because the next morning, I woke up in my bed with my boots on and no underwear, and there was half a sandwich in the fish tank. Not my worst night. But I can tell you from a long history of drinking, I can't swear in court to anything that happened after 11:36 p.m."

Amanda sighed. This just got complicated. Now, even Silver didn't have an alibi.

"I never met the dead diver. Oh, I like that/" He struggled to sit up and finally rolled to his side to pull a pad of paper and a pen out of a drawer in the coffee table. He scribbled a note that looked like a line drawing of a bird, and then he continued. "I got me one of those watches with the apps that tells you what you're doing, and my watch told me I was sleeping from 11:36 p.m. until 12:48. Or was it 2:48? 84? I'll ask my agent. I think he uses it to track me." Silver held a finger in the air to mark his points as he spoke. Slowly, his hand drifted to land on his chest.

He snorted.

Amanda stood up and inched closer to Silver, leaning over the man.

Unbelievable, he had fallen asleep. She had more questions, but they would have to wait. Quietly leaving the cabin, she pulled the door closed behind her.

Well, that was new information, but why did every answer on this case send her in a circle?

Back outside, she untied Qbert's leash, and they made their way to Ben's slip.

Crime scene tape was wrapped around the boat, keeping her from climbing aboard. Fortunately, she had a good view from the dock. She remembered how Robin had looked last night. There had been blood on her forehead and chest that had leaked out to cover the deck, but the woman lay face up, one of her arms at a strange angle.

Amanda walked around the boat, studying it from three sides. There were so many ways to trip and fall in a marina. Things on the deck to stumble over. Getting into the boats was always awkward, with ropes and moorings blocking the path. It was a wonder more people didn't end up hurt, but looking at the scene, Amanda could see no reason for Robin to have been on the top of Ben's boat unless she had been breaking in. The boat wasn't secure, with bilge pump hoses hanging like tentacles as they tried to keep it floating.

There was a commotion on the far side of the dock, and Amanda peeked around Ben's boat to see what it was.

Mrs. Erling was on the upper deck of her yacht. The wind had caught the bow of her bright-pink top, and the ends fluttered behind her as she gave directions to Marco and Jeffrey. In their crisp white uniforms, the crew hurried around the large boat, putting away equipment.

It looked like they were packing up. Did they plan to leave?

She had to let someone know.

THIRTY-FOUR

An Arrest

Amanda hurried Qbert toward the clubhouse. When she got far enough from the Erlings' boat, she pulled out her phone and dialed Detective Kim.

Off in the distance, a faint ring sounded.

Curious, Amanda stood on tiptoe and searched through the tall masts. The ring sounded again. Still faint.

When she was almost at the clubhouse, she heard the ring again, much closer now. Reaching out a hand to open the door that led into the marina offices, she snatched it back as the door flew open. Detective Kim exited with two officers leading a handcuffed Jack Roberts.

As they pushed past her, the manager protested loudly. "You got the wrong man! I just took the watch. It was sitting in his locker. I didn't kill anybody."

Sammy hurried out after them, the young woman's hands on her cheeks.

Amanda stepped up next to her. "What is happening?"

"They're arresting him. I don't know what to do. Should I call a lawyer? Do I need to close the club?" The girl wrung her hands together as if lathering soap then bit her knuckle.

Amanda watched Detective Kim put Jack in a car, and then he and the police officers left. She turned back to Sammy. "Did Jack ask you to call a lawyer?"

"No. I just thought that is what you were supposed to do, like in the movies. I don't even know a lawyer." Sammy flung her arms wide.

"Can you tell me what happened?" Amanda prepared herself to catch the young woman, who was blinking in slow motion. "Maybe you better sit down."

With one hand holding on to the railing by the entrance, Sammy folded her legs under her and sank to the concrete. She hung there for a second then shook herself and let go, settling cross-legged before she started talking. "Jack and I were having a marketing meeting, and a bunch of police came in and said they had a warrant. They searched the whole building and discovered Tobias's backpack in Jack's locker. Jack claimed he found it out in the marina, but everyone who works here knows Tobias always kept it in his locker, never really took it out. The big guy, the cute one in the suit, said they were taking him in for question, and Jack started talking."

"I heard Jack mention a watch as they were leaving."

"He admitted to stealing the backpack and says he found the watch in it but swears he didn't kill Tobias. I can't believe this is happening. I don't know what to do."

Amanda squatted down next to Sammy. "Is anyone else working?"

Sammy shook her head. "The gift shop is closed today, and the restaurant isn't open until dinner."

"Did you try calling someone for instructions?"

"None of the staff are answering their phones, and neither is the owner. No one else is expected until later today." The woman's face crumpled, and her perky ponytail drooped.

Amanda gazed over the marina. Once the police had left, the scene returned to its usual tranquility, interrupted only by the occasional call of a seagull or the sound of a boat departing, blending with the soothing lapping of the water. "Are there any events or appointments this morning?" she asked.

Sammy shook her head.

"Well, why don't you lock up for now? We'll put a note on the door saying there's been an emergency." Amanda glanced at the time on her phone as she made her suggestion.

Sammy scrambled to her feet, and Amanda followed, her knees cracking.

"That's a good idea." The young woman eyed the clubhouse door. "Would you go with me? I'm freaked out about being in there alone. I still can't believe Jack would hurt someone, but if he didn't do it, a killer is in the marina somewhere." Sammy glanced over her shoulder and shivered.

Amanda nodded. This was perfect. She could ask Sammy more questions and maybe even snoop around.

She sent Detective Kim a quick text about the Erling's leaving and moved to follow Sammy.

Qbert barked as she headed for the door.

Amanda looked down at the leash in her hand. "Can Qbert come, or should I tie him up out here?"

"Bring him. Extra defense."

Amanda looked down at Qbert, not sure how much defensive help he would be. He gave her a wide-eyed grin, his tongue sticking out of one side of his mouth.

Sammy held the door for Amanda and Qbert then closed and locked it behind them.

"How long have you worked here?" Amanda watched as Sammy hurried around, shutting windows and turning off coffeemakers and lights.

"It's just an internship for now, but I love sailing, and I wanted more time near the water before I start college in the fall. I'm majoring in oceanography." Sammy tugged closed the blinds and pulled drapes over the front windows.

"Do you have a lot of staff working here?"

"When the shop and restaurant are open, its busy. The chef and his staff will be here later setting up for a special dinner. It's usually just Jack and me in the early mornings. Robin and Tobias would be here, too, but they were always outside doing something." Sammy's shoulders slumped and tears welled up. "I can't believe they're both gone."

"You said the police found the backpack in Jack's locker. Does everyone have a locker?" Amanda cringed, realizing that was not the most subtle way to bring up the subject, especially while the young woman looked so vulnerable.

Sammy sniffed, then took a deep breath. "Come on. I'll show you." She led Amanda through the dining area and into the kitchen to a small room at the back. "These are the staff lockers. We usually start our shifts here or take breaks and eat. I just need to grab my purse, and then we can leave. Thank you so much for helping me lock up. It's a lot less creepy when someone else is here."

As Qbert sniffed the floor, searching for food, Amanda studied the lockers. They would hold some personal items and a change of clothes, but they were too small for a diver to keep their equipment in. "Did Tobias have another locker here or a dock box?"

Sammy tilted her head and studied Amanda. "Why are you asking about the lockers?"

Amanda fidgeted with Qbert's leash. "I should've told you to begin with. I think a clue might be stashed in either Tobias's or Robin's lockers that would help us figure out who killed them."

"But the police have already searched here."

"When I was asking Jack about memberships yesterday, he mentioned Tobias's locker in the clubhouse. He also said all the divers had storage boxes. Did the police search them too, or only look in the inside lockers?"

"There are storage boxes outside. I don't think the police looked at them, they aren't attached to the building." Sammy closed her locker and slung her purse over her shoulder then led Amanda outside and around to the back of the clubhouse, past kayaks, rental equipment, and trash cans, to a separate floating dock obscured by the pier above.

"I wonder why the police didn't search this area?"

"Probably didn't know it was owned by the clubhouse. The wharf noise gets loud so we just use it for dock boxes and lockers. Robin and Tobias kept their diving gear here."

"Robin was a diver?" Amanda almost dropped Qbert's leash. Why had she never considered that the marina had more than one diver?

"Tobias was the main one, and he did all the repairs with Mo. But Robin would back him up when needed. Here's Tobias's box." Sammy pointed to a vertical locker the size of a small closet.

Amanda tugged on the padlock, her shoulders slumping. Of course, it was locked.

Sammy nudged Amanda aside. "I can open it. I have Jack's keys. He has all the masters, so I didn't want to leave them sitting around." Sammy fished around in her purse until she found a big round key ring. Flipping through it, she located the key she wanted and slipped it into the padlock. It opened.

Amanda gave a little yip of excitement, catching Qbert's attention. He whined and jumped up on his hind legs, tail wagging. She patted the dog's head, pushed him off, and dropped his leash to open the lid.

The locker was a mess. Sun-faded equipment and tools jammed into corners and waterproof gear thrown to the floor instead of hanging on the neatly spaced hooks and shelves. A space showed where diving tanks and a wetsuit would have been stored. The floor was layered with faded waterproof dry bags. Amanda picked up a red one and looked inside: empty. She checked another one, this one blue. Nothing. Wait. She reached into the bottom of the sack and grabbed a slip of plastic. The bag was stamped with the words *TYME IRONLORE.*

"Do you know what this is?" Amanda waved the empty plastic bag.

Sammy shook her head.

"Can I take it?"

"Looks like trash to me." Sammy shrugged and then straightened. "Hey, I was supposed to be working all morning. Do you think they won't pay me with the club closed?"

Amanda kept her face neutral as she shoved the bag into her purse. It sounded like Sammy was getting past her shock and fear. "I don't know. Can we check Robin's storage box too?"

Sammy sighed then stomped to the other locker. Flipping through her keys, she unlocked the padlock and stepped aside.

Amanda left her contemplating her future paycheck while she sorted through the contents. It was similar to the first one and just as messy, only all the diving equipment seemed to be present. Hanging from a hook was a black wetsuit with a green stripe down the side that looked identical to the one Tobias was wearing when Amanda found him, except for the color of the stripe. Similar waterproof bags lined the bottom of the locker, but nothing was in them.

A noise sounded from the front of the clubhouse.

"I think that's the chef and his crew." Sammy's glum face lifted, and she hurried off, leaving Amanda alone.

Well, this had been a waste of time.

She dropped a handful of dry bags back to the floor, and something thumped. Squatting down, she reached into the back corner of the locker, peeling back the layer of bags.

A chill raced from Amanda's hairline to her toes. There on the floor, in a pile of wrinkled papers, lay a spear gun.

THIRTY-FIVE

Are You Safe?

As Amanda stared at the gun in the bottom of the locker, her mind spun. What did this mean? Had Robin killed Tobias? And if so, who had killed Robin?

Amanda realized she needed to call Detective Kim. She started to put everything back into the box the way she had found it then stopped. When she first arrived in town, she had called the detective about a body she had found, and by the time he arrived, it had disappeared, and the police didn't believe her. Better to not take chances this time.

Amanda leaned in to snap a photo. She pushed aside a page of the newspaper the gun was wrapped in, and it fell open to a story about the Channel Islands. Curious, she smoothed out the page. This wasn't a local newspaper. She tugged carefully at the page, hoping it wouldn't rip, until the paper's name was revealed: *San Diego Sunscape*.

What was a San Diego newspaper doing wrapped around a spear gun in a dead sailing instructor's locker box in Ocean Wood? Was this Robin's speargun? Had Amanda found the proof that Robin killed Tobias?

Amanda's hands trembled as she took several pictures of the gun and the position it was lying in the box. Then she returned everything back the way she had found it and sent a photo in a text message to Detective Kim. She sat back on the dock and was just lifting the phone to follow-up on her text when it rang.

"Where are you? Are you safe?" The curt voice of the detective straightened her spine.

Amanda gave her location and assured him she was safe. He promised to be right there.

After hanging up, Amanda shivered. She realized she was sitting alone, hidden behind a building and surrounded by dark shadowy water with the sound of cars driving on the wharf overhead drowning out all sounds but the sharp barks of sea lions.

Was she safe?

Keeping an eye on the storage box, Amanda moved out of the shadow of the wharf and closer to the club house to wait.

It didn't take long for Detective Kim and several officers to arrive. Amanda jumped up from where she was hugging Qbert and hurried to meet them.

"Did you touch anything?" Detective Kim asked.

"Well, yes, I touched a lot of things. I was searching the locker."

The detective groaned. "Gloves, Amanda. Gloves. Did you touch the gun?"

"No. *That*, I didn't touch." She pointed to the locker and explained how she had gotten access.

Detective Kim shook his head. "We didn't even know these were here. Okay. We'll take over. You can go." The detective snapped blue latex gloves into position.

"But can't I stick around and see what else you find?" Amanda flinched at his glare. "You wouldn't have the murder weapon if I didn't call you."

"Potential murder weapon." The detective sighed again, and Amanda was starting to hate that sound. "Amanda, you're friends with a person of interest in both a shooting death and a stabbing death. And you found the body both times. This doesn't look good for you or Ben. You need to leave. Don't worry. I'll find you later with questions. *Lots* of questions."

Amanda could see his point. She started to walk away then spun back. "Wait. So, Robin died from being stabbed?"

Detective Kim stared up and groaned. Then shook his head. "The Salinas ME determined she did fall, hard, and hit her head. But she was turned over after the fall and stabbed. That's what finally killed her. Someone really wanted her dead. It wasn't an accident. Now go." The detective waved off any further questions, and as he turned to where his police officers were spread out, searching all the lockers and boxes, he called over his shoulder, "Amanda, be careful."

As Amanda hurried around the front of the club-house, she could hear Sammy talking to someone, but not until she rounded the last corner did she see it was Captain Jeffrey Cook.

How many people lived in this marina, and yet every time she was here, she bumped into the skipper. For a second, she wondered if he was watching her, but she dismissed the suspicion as anxiety induced by her unusual morning.

"What's going on? Why are the police back?" Sammy frowned.

"I think they might have more questions." Amanda hurried past, tugging Qbert behind her. Sammy gawked, but the skipper caught her eye, and instead of his usual smile, he gave her a considering look.

THIRTY-SIX

Finally Breakfast

G rok wiggled into a more comfortable position as he reclined on the hood of the warm car he had found in the marina's parking lot. He kept his eyes open a slit to follow Amanda's approach. She waved and called him over. He ignored her. Finally, she came to him. When she got close enough, he asked, "Why is the skipper watching you?"

"Is he still watching? He was acting strange this morning. By the way, you won't believe what I found." Amanda bent over and peered at the front of the vehicle. "Hey, whose car is this? I think you're denting the hood."

Grok got to his feet then leapt to the ground. The metal made a popping sound as he left it. "Why, thank you for asking—yes, I did stay out all night. And, no, I'm not fine; I'm hungry."

"You're right. I should have asked. How are you? Did you find out anything last night?" Amanda squatted down and reached out. After he gave an imperious nod, she scratched behind his ears and ran a hand down his back.

Grok felt a rumbling purr roll up his chest, and he tamped it down. He was so weak when it came to skritches and pats. He usually just slapped her hand away to keep from making a fool of himself. This time he turned up his nose and walked past her with a sniff. "Oh, I found something. Take me for breakfast, and I shall tell you about it. I'd like their parmesan-crusted calamari. No, better yet, the lightly smoked wild California sardines."

"Where am I going to find that, and who's paying? Wait, where are you going?" Amanda called after him.

It was the opening Grok was looking for. He smiled over his shoulder, wiggling his whiskers. "Follow me."

Grok padded along the trail, hugging the coast until he got to a grand Queen Anne house with huge gable windows and a busy parking lot.

"What is this?" Amanda craned her neck to see in the expansive bay windows.

"A restaurant. The Fisherman's Feast. Their head waiter says they have the best breakfast menu in town. And inside is the man we are looking for." Grok purred in satisfaction; he was steps away from a hearty meal and had achieved the mission objective. It was turning into a good morning.

"You're amazing!" Amanda climbed the steps to the front door and stopped.

"What's wrong?" Grok scowled at the delay, his odor senses picking up the mix of spices in their seafood bisque. Should he have that instead?

"I can't take Qbert in there." Amanda glanced down at the shaggy dog.

Grok watched Qbert wag his tail then turn his dopey eyes up to the woman as he implored them to let him come. For a second, Grok thought Amanda was going to fall for the act.

"Wait a minute." Amanda followed a path through the front yard to a covered gazebo and tied the dog up inside.

"We'll be back soon, buddy," she promised.

The hairy beast whined as Amanda walked away until a butterfly fluttered past and grabbed the dog's attention.

If Grok were human, he would've rolled his eyes.

As they entered the fancy house, Grok shot through a side door and avoided the woman at the front taking names. Keeping to the shadows, he moved silently to the back of the restaurant. Amanda's loud steps clopped behind him, completely blowing the covert op. Easing around a potted plant, he had a line of sight with his prey. The bald man was still there.

"Excellent job. Now I have to figure out what to say." Amanda crouched beside him, making a ruckus as she pushed the vegetation aside. She studied the dark-suited man sitting at the table, his back to the wall.

Grok considered their options. Claws to the back of his knees would get him talking, and an ankle bite was also a strong motivator.

"Bother this. I'm just gonna go ask him." Amanda struggled to her feet and emerged from behind the plant to barge across the room to the bald man's table.

A waiter caught the movement—how could he have missed it?—and headed towards them.

Grok shook his head and padded after her.

"Hello there!" Amanda exclaimed as if she was surprised to see the bald man. As he looked up, she pulled out a chair and sat across from him.

Grok jumped up on the chair between them, his tail twitching in anticipation.

"Beat it." The man went back to his newspaper.

"I thought you wanted to talk."

"Don't know what you mean."

"Look, I'm really bad at games. I'll tell you what I know if you tell me what you know." Amanda gave the bald man an encouraging smile.

Grok hung his head. He never should have left this up to her.

The man dropped the newspaper and raised his eyebrows at Amanda.

A waiter arrived and swept Amanda with a disapproving stare. "Is this woman bothering you?" With a shake of the bald man's head, the waiter retreated.

"I'm listening." The big guy took his napkin, wiped each side of his mouth, and threw it on the table.

Grok growled at the aggressive gesture. This guy had been spending too much time watching mafia shows.

Amanda ignored the napkin and leaned forward. "Why do you want to find my sister? What was she doing for you?"

Grok could see Amanda's hands clenched in her lap, but he approved of the question. There was something softening in the man's posture as he considered talking to them.

The bald man leaned forward, steepling his fingers and putting his elbows on the table. The gesture pulled back the cuffs of his jacket and revealed an expensive-looking watch with a diamond face. He glanced dismissively at Grok then studied Amanda and gave a grim chuckle. "You really aren't Alexandra. You've got these big Bambi eyes that spill all your secrets. Alexandra is cunning and a shrewd investigator. Not seeing that in you."

"Yeah, well..." Amanda blew out a breath then shrugged. "Like I told you, I'm not her. My name is Amanda, and I'm trying to find her. What was she working on for you? Maybe it will help me track her down."

"Doubt it." He cocked his head.

Grok watched Amanda blink her eyes as they grew damp. He groaned. That was never going to work with this guy.

"Fine, all right. My name's Dom."

Grok whipped his head around to the guy who had fallen prey to the Bambi's eyes, whatever that was.

"I hired your sister to track down the history of a necklace. If she has skipped town, I want the necklace back. That's all you need to know." He spoke with a slight accent and drew out his words.

"She hasn't skipped town." Amanda frowned.

"Well, she isn't here."

Amanda sat back. Grok could tell she didn't know what to say to that. She made a terrible impression of thinking about what Dom had said and turned to Grok, eyebrows raised.

Knowing the man would just hear meowing, he instructed Amanda, "Ask him when he last heard from or saw her."

Amanda sat up and repeated Grok's question.

"My last contact with her was a couple of weeks ago. She was supposed to send weekly updates. I tried tracking her down when I didn't hear from her."

Grok considered this new information. His time with Alexandra was riddled with memory holes. She was a good investigator and rarely needed help. A stab of pain went through his head when trying to recall any details of her cases, and he quickly stopped probing the memory. Grok couldn't remember when he last saw Alexandra, what she was working on, or ever meeting this bald man before. "Ask him how they communicated."

Amanda repeated the question.

Dom looked from Grok back to Amanda then shrugged. "Mostly by phone, by email if she found something to share or had photos."

The man reached for his waist holster.

Grok was out of the chair, ready to attack, when Dom, not seeming to notice the huge cat on the table, pulled out his phone and started scanning. "Her last email was three weeks ago. She said she had a lead and would send me photos when she could. That's the last I heard from her."

Huh. That was a phone holster at his waist, not a gun.

Grok settled back in his chair and started to rethink his opinion of Dom.

"Did she give you any indication of where she was searching for information?" Amanda leaned forward now, oblivious to the near smiting that had almost occurred.

"Nah. Well, I got the necklace in the Santa Cruz Mountains, and she did want to check that out. But it's a big dead end."

"How do you know? Did you go look yourself?"

The man looked to either side to make sure no one was listening in then leaned forward. "Look, I'm just a luxury goods and jewelry dealer. My clients really get into this persona I got going on. But there's no way I could blend with the people where that necklace came from. And I have to know if it's the real deal without having my name tied to it. You get me?" Dom looked down at the finger he tapped on the table. "Your sister was the right person to look into it."

"Why her? Why not another investigator?"

The man smirked at Amanda. "How much do you know about your sister's business?"

Amanda searched her mind for what she had learned about Alexandra since she arrived in Ocean Wood, and it wasn't much. "She's a PI, a private investigator. She used to be a police officer."

Amanda's face creased as the man across the table stifled a laugh.

"A PI? Right. She's a paranormal investigator." The man drew out the last two words and watched Amanda's expression, not disappointed when she reeled back in her seat.

"A what?" Amanda shook her head. "That can't be right."

"I doubt she told her friends, but she was well-known in the circles. To be fair, she spent more time debunking paranormal stories than proving them. Guess you really didn't know her." Dom looked smug as he enjoyed Amanda's discomfort.

"I've talked to several of my sister's friends. They never mentioned her work."

Amanda seemed to lose herself in thought, so Grok applied a gentle claw to her leg to get her focus back.

"Ow! Ow-sey, okay, yep that was a surprise to learn about her." Amanda grabbed her leg and tried to play off her outburst.

"She had some powerful clients with a lot to lose if their names got out."

"What type of cases did she take? Do you know if she used codes in her work?"

"Nope. Now, you need to give me something. How can I reach Alexandra's partner? Maybe he knows the status of my case." Dom's glare was menacing as he leaned heavily on the table.

Grok hissed a warning. This guy was full of litter. Alexandra didn't have a partner. They needed to play it cool here so they could dig deeper.

"What?" Amanda's gasp had the people at the tables around them turning and staring. "A partner? I've never heard of her working with someone else except for Chief Rodriguez, her police partner."

Dom threw his napkin on the table, and his chair

squealed across the floor as he pushed it back and stood. "Well, she sure wouldn't share her side business with the police. This has been a waste of time. You and your sister are quite a pair. You're all fake innocence, riddles, and codes. But I'll tell you this... You better hope I hear from her by the time I finish my business here, or I'll be coming after you with my lawyer for the necklace."

As he spoke, he dipped his head towards Amanda. Grok watched as he unconsciously rubbed a hand over the expensive watch on his wrist.

"Ask him where he got the watch," Grok insisted.

Amanda repeated the question.

Dom stopped. His eyebrows drew up. He glanced at the watch on his wrist, and then he held it up for Amanda's view. "This? Bought it off a guy in town."

"You don't mind your clients seeing you in a fake watch?"

"Honey, unlike you, this is the real deal, an authentic Tyme Ironlore. The guy I got it from tried to pretend he was selling it for his father, but this model hasn't even been released yet."

Dom turned and left the room, angry footsteps pounding on the wooden floor.

THIRTY-SEVEN

Permission to Come Aboard

"My head is reeling." Amanda peeled back the lid on a can of sardines she had just purchased at the mini-mart and put the tin on the ground beneath the picnic table. Grok didn't like to eat on the floor, but she knew what was going to happen to that fish and didn't want to witness it at eye level.

Grok looked like he was going to continue the silent treatment he had been giving her since they left the restaurant without food. But the smell of fish seemed to repair his mood. "Yes, he did provide more than I had expected. We appear to be in the middle of a smuggling ring." He dipped his head into the can and returned with a fish in his mouth.

"What? I'm not talking about that. I mean, what he told us about Alexandra. That's she's a...a...you know."

"Obviously, I didn't know. At least, I don't remember knowing. I'm not even sure what a PI is." Grok plunged his face into the bowl and purred.

"A paranormal investigator?" Amanda paused while Grok was distracted. She waited until the cat lifted his head with a satisfied grin, fish and oil smeared from ear to ear. "It's someone that explores unexplainable events like ghosts or UFOs."

"Oh, I've seen the documentaries on your TV. Humans love learning about their cases. Is it not studied in school?" Grok licked his face clean while he waited for an answer.

Amanda sputtered. "It's not real. At least, I don't think it is. Those shows are for entertainment."

"Hmm. But how do they get the ghosts and aliens to act along with them? They are notoriously hard to direct." Grok dove back, face-first, into the bowl.

Amanda stared at the cat. "I don't even—no, just no. And who was this partner he mentioned? Did you ever see her working with someone else?"

Grok emerged and licked a big piece of fish off the end of his nose. "No. That is troubling. Alexandra might have made it up so that it looked like she had backup."

Amanda shook her head. She broke off another piece of cheese from a cheese stick and tossed it to Qbert then picked up the bottle of water she had bought for herself. "Maybe we need to focus on the other information he gave us. Do you think there really is a smuggling ring in town? There are a lot of new watches around."

Grok's face was buried back in the tin, and he didn't respond.

Amanda put down the bottle and grabbed her phone. After a minute of searching, she whistled. "I just looked it up." She waved her phone in front of Grok. "The name Dom gave us, which was also on the plastic bag I found in Tobias's storage box, is a luxury watchmaker, they aren't knockoffs."

"What are knockoffs?"

"Fakes that are made to look like the real thing. These are really pricey watches. I could buy a new grooming van with just one of them. Can you imagine wearing something that expensive around?"

"You drive something that expensive around."

"Whatever."

"Why would Tobias sell the watches as fake if he could make so much more with real watches? And why sell them here where everyone notices everything. Why not go to the city." Grok asked.

"That's a good point. Maybe Tobias stole the watches from someone else and didn't know they were real. If Dom had a genuine watch, then maybe the mayor's, Alan Erling's, and Jack's are real too and they don't know it."

Grok slurped as he chased the last morsels in the can. Finally, apparently satisfied he hadn't missed any, he sat up and licked his lips. "Jack said he found the watch in Tobias's locker, but what if he was involved in the smuggling? He had keys to everyone's lockers."

"So, he could have put the spear gun in Robin's locker after she was killed."

Grok considered what Amanda said as he cleaned his whiskers. "But I thought Jack had an alibi?"

"That's a little up in the air." Amanda explained Silver's inability to support Jack's whereabouts. "Either

Robin or Jack could have been the smuggler, or maybe they were in it together. You could move all kinds of things underwater, and no one would know. If Tobias stole the watches from them, they could have been searching for them. That would explain why he was killed. But why was Robin killed?"

Amanda's bottle thumped against the table as she put it down. "I found a diving suit almost identical to Tobias's in Robin's locker. Only this one had a green stripe; underwater, colors look different. Maybe someone thought they were killing Robin when they shot Tobias."

Amanda used both hands to pull at her hair. "You know, that newspaper is really bothering me. Where would someone get a San Diego paper?"

"The killer could have pulled it from the trash to hide the weapon." Grok settled back in the grass.

"Maybe, or the killer brought the newspaper with them from home. And there are people at the marina from San Diego."

"The Erlings."

"The Erlings travel all over. Maybe they smuggled the watches in. This could be big. Do you think we have enough to go to the police?" Amanda twisted her fingers together.

Tilting his head from side to side, Grok contemplated Amanda's question. "No. The police will say it's all coincidental. We can't prove it. The Erlings are important to this town. There's no way they'll accuse them of something without proof, and without searching the boat, they won't get it."

Amanda nodded. "Then we need to get on that boat and find proof before they leave."

As if summoning a solution, Amanda's phone rang.

She looked at the screen then turned panicked eyes on Grok "It's Luna Erling. How did she know we were talking about her?"

"She didn't, silly. Answer the phone." Grok lay back in a huff, keeping his eyes barely open to watch.

Amanda took a deep breath, shook herself, and then answered the phone. "Pink Power Wash and—"

"Oh, good, it's you. Rocky took us out to breakfast to apologize for the police's absurd request that we stay in town. Only now it's turned into a tour at Stone Beach and lunch." Luna Erling's voice was washed out by the sound of laughter and glasses clinking.

"Oka-a-a-y? What does—" Amanda wasn't sure where this was going but was cut off before she could ask.

"My precious girls are all alone on that big yacht and I can't find the skipper or Mateo, so you need to go check on them. The door's unlocked. Walk them, wash them. Whatever."

"Oh, Sure, but how—Oh, she hung up. How rude."

"What did she want?" Grok rolled forward.

Amanda looked across the parking lot to the marina. "Well, that was the interesting part. Luna Erling wants me to check in on Poppy and Daisy. They're all alone on the boat."

Grok let out a snort. "You have the most remarkable luck, unless she's setting you up."

"What do you mean?"

"Well, if she is the killer, she could be inviting you onto her boat to kill you, and then she can just tell everyone they thought you were breaking in."

"She did say the door was unlocked."

"Why would she leave the door unlocked with everything that's been happening at the marina? I'm going to come along and keep an eye on you."

At the marina gate, Amanda and Grok caught a fishing group exiting with armloads of tackle. Amanda held the door for them, and the last woman through nodded her thanks.

"Why didn't you ever ask Ben for the code that lets you in?" Grok strutted down the dock towards the Erlings' boat.

"I have this feeling that at some point the police will pull the entry records, and I don't want them to know how often I'm here."

Grok stopped and turned to her.

"What?"

"For a minute there, you sounded exactly like your sister."

Amanda was inordinately pleased by the compliment. Her step took on an extra skip as they made their way towards the largest vessel in the marina.

She retrieved her phone from her purse and dialed

Ben's number, which went to voicemail. "Hi Ben, it's Amanda. Luna Erling just asked me to dog sit. I suspect someone on their boat was smuggling watches. Unfortunately, I don't have any proof, so I'm going aboard to look around. I thought someone should be informed besides Grok." Amanda hesitated, unsure what else to say. "Thanks," she added and then hung up. She tucked her phone into her back pocket.

"Not a bad idea since no one would understand me if I tried to tell them what happened." Grok sniffed the air.

Amanda scrutinized the yacht. No lights illuminated its interior, but seeing more than that through the tinted windows was impossible.

"Hello?" Amanda called out then knocked on the side of the vessel.

"That's not how you do it. Say the thing," Grok demanded.

Amanda frowned at the cat, who narrowed his eyes and stared so intently that she was sure he was reaching into her mind to make her do his bidding. "I won't do it."

"I feel a fit of singing coming on." A low crooning meow gargled up from Grok's throat.

"What is that?" Amanda put her hands over her ears. "Why are you making that noise? It's horrible. Stop. I'll say the thing."

Grok abruptly quit singing. "I'm waiting."

"Permission to come aboard?" Amanda called out in a loud sing-song voice.

"Skipper," Grok added.

"*Skipper!*" Amanda yelled loudly.

Grok erupted in laughter; his leg collapsed, and he rolled onto his back, gasping for breath. "That was fabulous. Can you do it again?"

"Shush. You're ridiculous." Amanda glared at the cat writhing on the dock while she waited for a response from the yacht.

None came.

"They can't understand me anyway. You're the crazy one talking to a cat." Grok sniffed and gracefully flipped to his paws.

"I don't think anyone is here. Why don't you find a lookout place and let me know if you see anyone." Amanda scanned the boat. Luna said the dogs were alone, but she still worried someone would be there.

Grok whacked Amanda with his tail. "Having a lookout is a good idea, but how can I alert you if someone is coming? I can't exactly phone you." Grok sat on his haunches on the dock, waiting for Amanda's response.

"If you make that horrible singing sound again, I'm sure I'll hear it."

Grok sniffed and turned away.

THIRTY-EIGHT

Look Out

G rok settled on a boat berthed two away from the Erlings' yacht. Half the size of the yacht, the boat had a tall tower and a comfortable chair that provided a vantage point over the boatyard.

The boat was undergoing maintenance. Canvas sheets covered much of its furniture, and a long sheet draped from the tower, making it easy to climb. The workers appeared to have temporarily stepped out for lunch, leaving the deck scattered with tools, trays full of paint, dirty brushes, and paint cans.

The timing was perfect, as Grok didn't plan on staying long. At least, he hoped not. Amanda better be quick searching and picking up the dogs. Grok assessed that the chance of finding something tying the Erlings to watch smuggling was low, and the odds of getting caught were high.

Scanning the marina showed very few people around. The clubhouse was closed today, probably because the police still had the marina manager in custody. The lot served as overflow parking for nearby restaurants, but he didn't recognize anyone milling about.

The plastic seat creaked as he settled deeper into his vigil over Amanda. She required more work than her sister.

Alexandra was very independent. She rarely asked for his help on a case. Her time with the police and as an investigator had made her tough, a bit hard sometimes. It wasn't unusual for her to leave him alone for weeks at a time, though never this long before. His species didn't do well alone. While she hadn't needed Grok's help, she had given him a warm place to live and food. And now she was missing.

Grok felt a tightness in his chest. He had failed Alexandra. He would not fail her sister. He closed his eyes at the pressure in his head.

In the weeks before Alexandra disappeared, she had become very secretive, making notes in her casebook. Grok thought she was following a case. He'd seen her packing her car the night before and assumed she would call him when ready to go. But the next time he woke, she was gone.

What was she working on?

Grok felt himself slipping. He stretched and tried to shake himself out of the reaction. He dug in his claws as his vision blurred. Blinking, he realized digging into his memories was triggering one of his attacks. He couldn't black out now. He was looking out for Amanda. His last thought was that he had to take better care of her than he had of her sister, and then his world went black.

Something tickled Grok's nose as he regained consciousness. A cool breeze buffered his body. He became aware of a sharp pain in his claw and the bewildering sense of not knowing where or when he was.

When he blinked his eyes open, a butterfly sitting on the tip of his nose filled his vision. As it flittered away, he saw his arm stretched taut, two claws caught in fabric above his head. That explained the pain. Without thinking, he retracted his claws.

Grok let out a howl as his body dropped.

He tried to use his claws to latch on to the cloth again, but they refused to respond. He managed to roll onto his back in time to launch into the air.

Seeing what lay ahead, he swam backward through the air. As his limbs windmilled, time stilled and his mind floated. Images of him flying to a vast space station, cats everywhere, walking on their hind legs, and talking to each other. A sense of freedom. A vision of a prison cell. Cats forced through a fiery ring of light. Grok clung to the image; it was important, but it was too late. He was out of time.

The images disappeared. His limbs were windmilling, and he wasn't able to brace himself. He landed with a crash in the work area on the deck below.

THIRTY-NINE

The Search

Getting on board was easy. Getting inside was another matter.

Standing on the swim platform at the back of the yacht, Amanda tugged on the door to the crew cabin. Locked.

Climbing the stairs to the next deck, she tugged on the patio doors. The automatic sensor that had swished them open on her previous visits now kept them locked tight.

She hesitated at the foot of the external ladder leading to the third level and listened. A light wind gently rocked the boats around them, metal pulleys striking the masts like a chorus of chimes. Several docks over, a family was bringing in their boat after a morning on the bay. A maintenance crew was hosing down the pier near the gate, calling out to each other as they worked.

But not a sound came from the Erlings' yacht.

Amanda climbed the stairs to the top level. Most of

this section was open but devoid of personal items. She tried the door and windows—everything was locked.

It occurred to Amanda that one of the windows on the deck below might have been left open. Getting on her hands and knees, she held on to the railing and leaned over the side of the boat to check the windows on the level below.

Something moved against her leg.

Amanda jerked and cried out; the sound cut off as her hand slipped. Her face smacked into the composite panel, burning as it slid. Hand flailing, she caught the railing and regained her balance.

Leveraging her torso back up, she collapsed on the wooden deck, her arm over her eyes while she caught her breath. Finally moving, she squealed as two hairy faces with bulbous eyes stared down at her.

"Poppy? Daisy?" The little Pekingese dogs wagged their tails. "How did you guys get out here?"

The two dogs yipped excitedly and took off. Amanda fumbled to her feet and followed on weak legs. The dogs easily descended the stairs to the lower level, apparently not needing a human to carry them. On the main deck, they hurried to the patio doors. In the blink of an eye, they disappeared.

Amanda rushed over to the wall of glass. There, cut into the patio door, was a dog door with a rubber seal around it. The color of the rubber seamlessly blended with the main door. She examined the hole, pushing it open to see how far the flap would go. Could she make it?

A seagull squawked overhead. She looked up and

considered her options. She could try to lure Poppy and Daisy out, but she really wanted to look around inside, and technically, she had been given permission—not to snoop, but to go inside. She knew the Erlings were getting ready to leave, only staying because the police had asked them to after Robin's murder. She also knew they were close to the mayor and Detective Kim couldn't investigate them without hard evidence. Where better for a killer to hide?

Now that Jack had no alibi, would the police remove Ben as a person of interest or try to save face and work harder to find a motive for him? Even if they couldn't find one, the cloud of suspicion would stain Ben's career and he wouldn't stay in Ocean Wood.

Amanda had no idea why she had this feeling in her gut that if the Erlings left, they would never find the killer. She was a dog groomer, not a psychic cop, but something on this yacht had always felt off to her.

Making up her mind, she dropped her purse from her shoulder and forced it through the flap. Her arms went through easily. Pushing her head into the opening, the flap rested on the back of her neck. The next part was awkward, but she managed to inch her shoulders, chest, and waist through the door.

Her hips were a problem, as they had been most of her life. Amanda regretted putting her phone in her back pocket, she could feel it catch on the frame. Wiggling two fingers between her hip and the frame, she freed the phone and tossed it onto the floor next to her purse. Using her feet outside to push, she wiggled like an inchworm until her hips burst through.

Falling forward, her chin smacked the deck, and one foot was still hanging out the door. She drew it in as she rolled onto her back and gasped for breath. Maybe that hadn't been a good idea.

Amanda closed her eyes. A tongue licked a wet strip up her neck to her ear.

"Ack!" She gently pushed the dogs away and, rolling over, rose to her knees. Grabbing her purse, she knee-walked across the space until she got to the dinette and used it to pull herself to standing.

Feeling an intense sense of urgency, Amanda didn't wait to catch her breath. She started searching drawers in the kitchen and storage spaces in the dinette area. Matchbooks, spare blankets, extra dishes—nothing raised any red flags, though she wasn't sure what evidence of smuggling would look like. Maybe a bag of watches? A knife or spear gun with a label that said *murder weapon*?

She moved on to the living room. She found a drawer with dog stuff—leashes, water bowls, and extra food. She would come back to that. Another drawer was full of books, primarily bestsellers, some memoirs, and some on sailing. But besides that, there was a surprising lack of personal items.

There were many storage compartments in the helm, most holding charts and logbooks—a weird calculator, some foreign coins, but nothing notable.

Amanda headed down the stairs to the cabins. Poppy and Daisy bounced along behind her, excited by the new visitor.

She paused, unsure of which way to go. Pushing

open the closest door, she got lucky. It looked like the main cabin. One side of the bed was obviously Alan's. The watch she had seen him wearing was on the bedside table. She hesitated as she pulled open the drawer beneath it, not sure what to expect. There was a bottle of heart medicine and a boring document folder. Amanda pulled it out and flipped through the contents, suddenly stopping on a page. It was a bill of sale for a 145-foot yacht. Hadn't the skipper said they preferred to use the large yacht back in San Diego? Was this the same vessel? If so, why had Alan Erling sold it? The rest of the documents were bills, including a past-due mortgage statement. It looked like the Erlings were in very deep financial trouble.

Amanda returned the folder to the drawer and did a quick scan of Alan's narrow closet, with hanging clothes and a set of golf clubs.

Luna's side of the room was more cluttered: natural supplements, homeopathic and aromatherapy bottles, a yoga mat, and a closet crammed full of clothes. Nothing triggered Amanda's Spidey senses.

Backing out to the hall, she checked the other doors and found several bedrooms that appeared to be uninhabited, with neatly made beds and empty drawers and several storage areas.

How could anyone travel with so little stuff? Her RV was stacked from floor to ceiling with items—everything she left Ohio with, most of which had to be moved before she could see a client. Maybe they had taken everything to the hotel they were staying in.

But what about the crew? They were the ones who spent most of their time on the boat.

At the back of the hall, she found a hatch-style door and a narrow set of stairs. Poppy and Daisy insisted on following along, and the path led the three of them down through a small engine room.

Stopping and checking every storage compartment she passed took time. Most were full of food, equipment, or emergency gear.

Outside the engine room in a small pathway that led to the crew cabins, Poppy and Daisy started to bark. They clawed at a compartment near the floor. Amanda got on her hands and knees and opened the metal latch. The compartment was empty. She tried the close the door, but Poppy blocked her and Daisy dove inside. Attacking the back wall, she clawed at it until one corner popped up.

"What have you got there, girl?" Amanda pushed the small dog back and took over, prying the panel up. Behind it was a deep, low cable run, and tucked behind the plastic-coated wires and hoses, she spotted something blue. Reaching in, she pulled it out, being careful of the cables. "This what you're looking for?"

The dogs hopped over each other, sniffing the PVC dry bag.

Amanda ran a hand over the broken white wave-shaped logo printed in white ink. "This is the same bag I saw on Robin's boat."

She shifted on to her knees and, hearing Detective Kim's voice in her head, got a pair of latex gloves from her purse, pulling them on before setting the bag up.

It felt heavy. There was something round and hard in the bottom. Unlatching and unrolling the top, she angled the opening of the bag towards the light, but it was still too dark. Reaching in, she felt around. There was definitely a rock in the bag, along with something else. She pulled the other item out.

The small dogs whimpered as she pulled out a black neoprene diver's glove wrapped in a spotted white cloth. Not a cloth—a shirt. A white uniform shirt, and it was stained brown.

That was dried blood.

Amanda sat back hard, slamming into the narrow walkway and startling the small dogs. Their whimpers turned to growls. The dogs looked towards the crew cabin then took off running the opposite direction.

Amanda heard it too. The click of a latch. Scrambling to her feet, she shoved the neoprene glove and the shirt back into the bag and closed the compartment door.

Clutching the dry bag to her chest, the rock thumping against her stomach, she ran down the hall, back through the engine room, and up the hatch to the cabin area.

Daisy and Poppy were waiting at the hatch. They whined and nipped at her, jumping on her legs, their little paws padding softly on her knees.

"Someone's coming, girls. I have to hide," Amanda whispered to the dogs.

Neither seemed to understand her. Then Poppy's ears flicked up. She turned and sniffed, tilting her head as she listened, and a low growl came out of her throat. Amanda headed for the stairs to go up to the living room and galley area. Maybe she could make it out the dog door again before anyone saw her.

The person following her moved faster. Amanda could hear them coming through the hatch.

Poppy and Daisy bounded up the stairs past her. They raced towards the sofa in the living room, but instead of jumping onto it, they ran behind it. Amanda dived into the space behind them. While roomy for two small dogs, the cramped corner did nothing for Amanda's back, but she was completely concealed from the rest of the cabin, for now.

A man's voice broke the silence. "I know you're in here. Why are you running?"

FORTY

Fur Tornados

The dogs whined beside Amanda.

"Shut up, mutts!" The man's voice tracked with footsteps crossing the room. Cabinet doors opened and slammed. A door opened; Amanda thought it was to the helm. She peeked her head up and saw the back of a man stepping out of the room.

Maybe this was her chance.

Before she could move, his footsteps returned, and she ducked down.

Keys jingled over by the patio doors. "What do we have here? Did someone lose their phone?"

Amanda choked back a gasp. She remembered pulling her phone out of her pocket when she crawled in. How had she forgotten it?

"Amanda, I know you are here. Luna sent me over after she talked to you." As the man spoke, he was in the galley, opening and slamming doors.

Amanda wondered if she should stash the dry bag

under the couch and pretend this was all a misunderstanding. She tried, but the couch was a solid platform with the built-in storage.

Something broke nearby, followed by a curse. Then the man continued calling her name.

Footsteps grew closer to Amanda's hiding spot.

The voice stopped, along with Amanda's heart. The dogs panted softly beside her.

The cushions flew back. "Gotcha."

Exposed, Amanda scrambled to her feet.

Captain Jeffrey Cook in his pristine white uniform smiled his toothpaste grin at her. "What were you doing?"

Amanda opened and shut her mouth twice before finally blurting out, "I was chasing the dogs, trying to get them to come out for a walk." The well-behaved dogs sat at her feet. No chasing needed.

Amanda's arms ached as she held the dry bag with the heavy stone behind her back.

"Well, you're not going to be a very successful dog expert if you can't even handle those two." The skipper held out a hand.

Amanda bypassed the offer and skirted around him, keeping her back away from him. As she did her purse bumped a cabinet and fell off her shoulder. The added weight tore the dry bag from her fingers, and it dropped to the deck with a hard thump.

The smile disappeared from the skipper's mouth like a wiper across a windshield. "Well, now, that is a shame. This changes everything."

"Where did that come from?" Amanda's voice squeaked.

As the captain stared at the bag, Amanda could feel her pulse throbbing in her throat, the rhythm out of pace with the long silence. His brows lowered, and a shark-like sneer warped his features. "I suppose I shouldn't be surprised you figured it out."

The look on the captain's face told her it was too late. Maybe she could throw him off guard. "Why did you do it? Was smuggling watches so profitable you didn't want to share?"

The skipper gave a deep choking laugh. "Sure, it was a lucrative business. Robin and I had a system. I bring in the timepieces from my travels. She had connections with a distributor in San Francisco, and we both made a nice bundle of cash. Better retirement plan than we were ever going to get wiping our rich bosses a—"

Poppy growled at the skipper as he stepped forward.

Amanda took a nervous step back, almost tripping over the bag. "So, what happened? Did Tobias steal the watches and start to sell them?"

"See, I knew you were clever. That fool thought they were knockoffs, was selling them for a fraction of their worth. Imagine my shock when I saw my watches being worn around town by the most distinguished members of Ocean Wood's society."

"And so, you killed him." Amanda took a step backward as the captain looked away.

"Not my fault he crossed a line. He didn't even have the watches on him. His dry bag was empty."

"So, you and Robin took every opportunity to search the marina for them."

"Very good." The skipper stepped closer.

Poppy and Daisy issued a sharp bark in warning. He turned to look at them.

With her heart racing, Amanda took advantage of the distraction. Snatching the dry bag off the floor, she ran for the sliding glass doors.

"Freeze." The skipper's voice came out hard.

Amanda spun around and saw an orange gun in his hand. He chuckled. "A flare will do as much damage as a bullet when it hits you, and it's an easier accident to explain."

Amanda swallowed. She couldn't stop herself from falling back a step.

The skipper raised the gun.

Suddenly, twin fur tornados leapt across the couch, using the springs to catapult higher and attack. Amanda wouldn't have believed it if she hadn't seen it herself.

With gnashing teeth, Poppy and Daisy flew through the air and landed with a snarl on the captain, biting down on material and skin.

The skipper screamed.

Amanda bolted for the door, and it slid open. She rushed outside. Sneakers beat across the deck as she scrambled for the stairs. Losing her footing, she fell half the distance. At that exact moment, a flare shot across the space where her head had been.

"Get off me!" The skipper rushed from the cabin, swinging in a circle to dislodge the dogs hanging like sandbags from his legs. Amanda winced and almost turned back as she heard a thump.

Reaching the swim platform, she scrambled for the dock. Her balance was off. Her arms windmilled wildly.

Hands grabbed her shirt and belt, pulling her onto the dock.

Amanda looked up. "Help! He's trying to kill me!"

Ben and Chief Rodriguez had grabbed fistfuls of her shirt, pulling her back from the edge. Detective Kim and several officers passed them at a run as they boarded the boat, guns drawn.

There was a scuffle, the flair gun was kicked aside, and soon, the officers had the skipper in handcuffs.

"Poppy? Daisy?" Amanda pulled away from Ben and called for the dogs. She tried to re-board, but two furry heads popped over the railing before she could. They yipped and raced down the stairs to Amanda, quickly jumping the gap to the deck.

Amanda knelt on the dock and greeted them. "My heroines!"

The dogs jumped onto their hind legs and leaned into Amanda, licking her hands as she tried to pet them.

"Amanda, I was so worried when I got your voicemail. What happened?"

Ben crouched beside Amanda, and the dogs sniffed and yipped their interest in him.

There was a commotion, and Detective Kim and several officers led a struggling Jeffrey Cook off the boat.

Daisy and Poppy growled.

The dogs lunged for the skipper's feet as he passed. He

stumbled to avoid them, kicking out their direction. Detective Kim tightened his hold and yanked him back.

Ben and Amanda caught the Pekingese's collars and stopped them from following the arrest and exacting their own justice.

Their prey was instantly forgotten, and they launched themselves at Amanda, yipping their excitement.

FORTY-ONE

Mystery Solved

"What is going on here?" Disapproval was heavy in the mayor's voice.

Everyone spun towards the city official picking his way through the police as he headed for them.

"Where are you taking my captain?" Alan Erling asked, his head visible behind the mayor. He looked down at the shorter man. "Rocky, are you going to do something about that?"

The captain turned his charming smile Rocky's direction. "This is all a misunderstanding. Amanda is not very stable right now. She put herself in danger, and I was just trying to help out."

"Are you kidding? You were trying to set me on fire!" Amanda's voice wavered.

Ben gasped and tried to pull Amanda behind him.

"Mayor Shore." Chief Rodriguez inclined her head. "We're in the process of taking everyone down to the station, where I'm sure we can sort this all out."

"Then you're going to want this," Amanda held the dry bag out to the chief.

"What is that?" the woman asked, refusing to take the bag. She looked over at Detective Kim.

Amanda's arm grew heavy, and she dropped it to her side while she waited for the detective to hand the skipper off to another officer and put on a pair of latex gloves. He took the bag from Amanda, nodding approvingly at her gloved hands, and looked inside.

Detective Kim jerked his head back, eyebrows winging up, then pulled enough of the blood-stained white shirt from the bag to show the others.

"It even has his name on it," Amanda offered.

"No, not the skipper..." Mr. Erling shook his head in denial.

"Another one of your bad judgement calls," came a tart voice from behind the man.

"Yes, Mother." Mr. Erling flinched and stepped aside to show a thin woman in a silk pantsuit giving a disapproving sniff.

Amanda leaned closer to Detective Kim. "I was on Robin's boat yesterday and saw this bag. She tried to hide it from me. I think she knew the skipper had killed Tobias and was keeping the glove as proof or protection from him. As some point, he must have decided she was more of a risk then an asset. But when he killed her, he must have gotten blood on his uniform shirt. With the police watching everything that happened at the marina after that he couldn't get rid of it. So, his only option was to get the Erlings to leave and once they were far enough out, drop the shirt over the side with the rock."

Luna Erling pushed her way around her husband, bumping Mayor Shore, who wobbled on the deck. She rushed to Amanda. "Are my babies hurt?"

"They were so brave. They showed me where the evidence was hidden and attacked the skipper when he came after me. Daisy and Poppy saved me." Amanda handed the Pekingese off to her.

"My little warriors." Luna Erling kissed the top of each dog's head then turned back to the group. "But I don't understand why the skipper would kill Tobias."

Amanda explained how the skipper and Robin were smuggling in contraband watches. "He told me Tobias intercepted a package of watches and started selling them around town." Amanda frowned. "But I think Tobias hid them and they've been trying to find them ever since. Grok even heard them talking about it in the pub."

Everyone turned to look at Amanda.

"I mean that Grok and I overheard two people in hoodies talking about searching for something, but we didn't know who they were. You didn't find any other watches when you searched Tobias's things, did you?" She looked towards the detective.

Detective Kim shook his head. "No, we didn't know about them. Smuggling does explain some of the other evidence we found, like large deposits and withdrawals in Robin's bank account going back more than a year and bags of cash on her boat."

"They must have brought in dozens at a time. There's

no way Tobias could've sold all of them to people in Ocean Wood without drawing attention. I know nothing about luxury watches but noticed the mayor's and Mr. Erling's right away. They stand out."

The mayor made a strangled sound. "I've never bought anything illegal. As I've said before, this was a gift from my daughter." he straightened his tie. Realizing the move exposed his wrist, he put his arm down and pulled a cuff over his glittering timepiece.

"I don't know anything about a watch." Mr. Erling clamped a hand down on his wrist.

His mother made another tsking sound. "I'll contact the lawyer."

Amanda didn't think she should mention Dom's watch. She looked at the detective. "Jack said he took a watch from Tobias's locker. Did you find any other clues there?"

"Originally we checked the locker inside the clubhouse and had surveillance on it, so we knew when Jack stole the watch. We've also thoroughly checked the outside storage lockers you found and didn't find anything," the detective confessed.

Amanda rubbed her chin. "So where are the rest of the watches?"

"I can help with that." Mo stepped forward, dressed in faded jeans and a worn T-shirt with her tool bag over her shoulder. "We found what put a hole in your boat, Ben."

Unfazed by the uniforms, she elbowed over to Ben and pulled a package from her bag. "This was on the bottom of your boat. Whoever put it there punctured the hull. That's why you were taking on water."

Ben reached for the plastic-wrapped dry bag.

Both the chief and Detective Kim shouted, "No!"

Jerking back, Ben threw his hands in the air. "I can't believe I almost touched it. What was I thinking?"

"Good thing you didn't." The detective had the first dry bag in an evidence bag and turned it over to an officer before he put on a new pair of gloves and accepted the second one, which looked almost identical.

He opened the waterproof bag, unrolling the top, and reached inside. He pulled out a fistful of glittering watches. "There are about forty or fifty in here."

"Would someone kill for that?" Ben leaned in.

"If those are real, then that bag is worth millions," Amanda told him.

"What?" Ben whipped his head towards her.

Chief Rodriguez groaned. "Looks like you were involved in the case all along and didn't know it."

Securing the top of the bag, Detective Kim turned to the mayor and Mr. Erling. "I'll expect you gentlemen and your watches at the station before closing today to make your official statements."

The mayor fluttered his hand as he sputtered out a protest. "We happen to have a meeting this afternoon about a donation for the park. I'm sure this can all wait. We are both very busy men with the highest reputations to protect. We would never be involved in something like—"

Chief Rodriguez cut in. "Come on, Rocky, you know

we have to ask questions now so there are no questions later when you're running for reelection."

Mayor Shore frowned.

"We'll be there this afternoon." Alan Erling made a slashing movement to the mayor when he tried to protest again.

"Has anyone seen Grok?" Amanda didn't mention he was supposed to be on lookout. She searched the neighboring boats for him.

"Is that your cat?" Mo pointed then recoiled as she looked at the animal hobbling towards them.

"Grok!" Amanda rushed to the cat but was afraid to touch him.

One side of his fur was covered in blue paint, and his feet looked like someone had dipped them in frosting. He left a trail of white paw prints.

Grok let out a low guttural noise of displeasure, flinching when Amanda pulled a ball of wadded-up tape off the side of his head.

"What happened?" Amanda asked, forgetting they had an audience.

Mo put her hands on her hips. "I'll tell you what happened. The team working on the Beck's boat didn't clean up again, and Grok found his way into the mess. Get him off my dock; I don't want to have to sand out more paint!" Mo stalked off to give someone a stern talking-to.

Luna had slipped onto the boat and returned with several large beach towels. "Here. Keep them; we owe you after you've helped us out of this mess."

"Come on. I'll give you a ride home," Ben offered.

Amanda wrapped the towels around Grok, careful to cover all the paint.

"Don't worry, big guy. I saw mineral oil at home—or rather, at Alexandra's house. That will take this paint right off." She gently lifted the heavy cat, fumbling slightly to adjust the weight. Grok started to relax in her arms. "There you go. I've got you. I won't let you down."

FORTY-TWO

Chasing Butterflies

"She looks beautiful," Katrina exclaimed as she entered the back room and ran her hand over the cream-colored Afghan Hound's hair.

Amanda stepped back and admired her work. The dog, Angel, was always challenging and never lived up to her name, but she loved working on her. Her owner had become a regular client. Amanda playfully tapped the big nose with her finger, and the dog chased the finger until her lead pulled her back.

"I can't thank you enough for letting me work here, but is it keeping you from hiring someone new?" Amanda braced herself as she lifted the heavy dog to the floor and attached her to a lead in the corner next to Grok's kitty bed.

The big cat eyed the hairy dog suspiciously then rolled onto his back and ignored her.

"To tell you the truth, it's been a relief not to manage anyone. I wanted to provide the service for my clients but having you in town means they have access to a good groomer, and I don't have to provide one." Katrina flicked a long blonde hair off the sleeve of her jacket.

"Well, I appreciate it," Amanda replied, sweeping the hair off the table and wiping it down with a towel.

"So, I'm heading out. Can you lock up behind you?" Katrina pulled on her jacket and slung a bag with the Best Friends Boutique logo onto her shoulder.

Amanda agreed and gave the woman a wave goodbye before returning to her cleanup.

As she rinsed the tub, Amanda started thinking about her sister's casebook. Something Dom said about her sister liking puzzles and writing in code had stuck in her mind. She had been reading about substitution ciphers and knew they had to be the answer. She just needed to find the key.

"Grok, do you know if my sister ever spoke to you about codes or keys?"

"Keys are in the bowl by the door," Grok muttered as he rolled over and looked at Amanda with sleepy eyes.

"I'm not talking about house keys. I'm talking about —never mind," Amanda saw the cat's eyes were closed again.

She finished with the sink and moved on to sweeping up the floor.

The bell rang on the front door. Amanda put down her broom and hurried to the front room. Anh from the travel agency was fiddling with the shelf of rubber toys near the door.

"Hello, Amanda. I'm here to see if you plan to keep your sister's office or if we should find another sub-tenant.

You're paid until the end of the month, but we're heading out on vacation in a week and need to settle the contract. Do you want it transferred to your name?"

"I'm not sure when Alexandra is going to come back. I don't want to close her office or transfer it to my name. But I can pay the electric bill now that I have steady clients here." Amanda straightened a set of water bowls on the shelf as she waited for his answer.

Anh tilted his head. "I'll have to ask Amy; she's in charge, but I'm fine with that. We can talk again when we get back from our vacation."

Amanda was relieved. She didn't want to let her sister down, and closing her office seemed like something she would be disappointed in.

Anh waved goodbye, and she locked the door behind him then hurried to the back room to finish cleaning up.

"Come on, Grok. It's time to go. We're gonna be late to Ben's again." Amanda put on her jacket, slipped her purse over her shoulder, and flicked off the lights while waiting for Grok by the front door.

"I'm hungry," Grok declared as he finally came into the room and padded toward the front door.

"Of course you are. Ben said he'll have food at his boat-warming party." Amanda gave the cat a light push to get his bum over the threshold, and then she turned and locked the door behind her.

Grok hissed and swatted at her hand. "I'm moving faster than you do without coffee in the morning." The cat stretched in a downward dog pose and kneaded his claws on the concrete.

As Amanda hurried down the sidewalk, trusting Grok was moving at his own pace behind her, a series of butterflies chasing each other fluttered in front of her. She smiled wide; something about the them always lightened her heart. Or maybe they were familiar and a part of her life now that she was finally starting to feel like she had a place in Ocean Wood.

FORTY-THREE

Boat Warming

Everyone else had already arrived by the time they got to Ben's boat at the marina.

Albert had set up his wheelchair at the edge of the dock so he could comfortably talk to everyone sitting around the table in the stern of the boat. Dot was just passing him a drink when they arrived. "Amanda, there you are." She called out, "Ben, Amanda's here."

Ben emerged from the interior of the boat with a platter of appetizers. He laid them in the center of the table in front of Frank and then held out a hand to help her over the edge. "Welcome aboard. Would you like a tour?"

Amanda nodded and followed Ben into the interior of the boat. It was very different from the last time she saw it, covered in buckets and hoses.

Ben raised his left hand and swept it slowly in an arc as he spun, noting the spaces. "There's the galley, the dining/office area, all my storage. The chair is my sofa. And up there is the cockpit."

"I like what you've done with the place now that its dry and the bilge pumps aren't running. It's cozy." Amanda nodded her support.

"Thanks." Ben tugged at the button at his neck.

"Hey, want to see something?" Amanda called to Qbert, and the dog bounded towards them.

Ben tilted his head and frowned as Amanda shut them into the cabin and asked, "When did you put this latch on the door? It doesn't match the rest of the boat."

"The salt air had rusted the old one, I installed the lever as soon as I took possession. Mo says I'm going to need to do something else there."

Amanda grabbed a bag of treats off the counter and balanced one on the door handle. The dog lunged for the treat, pawing at the handle until it dropped, and the door swung open. "Yeah, that might be a good idea."

Ben put a hand over his mouth, "I didn't know he could do that. At least he can't get off the boat."

Amanda called out to Albert, "Can you call Qbert?"

Albert let out a whistle. Ben squawked as Qbert nimbly jumped the edge of the boat, unconcerned about the gap to reach the slice of deli turkey Albert held out for him.

"I think that is how you ended up with Tobias's glove in your bedroom. Sometime between when Tobias was killed and Robin took the bag, one of the gloves must have fallen out, and Qbert brought it to you as a gift."

"That stinker. I thought he couldn't get off the boat.

I'm going to have to dog proof the whole place." Ben flung his hands up. "At least now I know he's here because he likes it. He seems to love lounging on the hull and watching birds and the action at the marina."

Amanda glanced out the front of the boat and saw Grok spread out on the warm wood of the hull soaking up the last of the day's sun. She shivered. She didn't have the same ease around dead bodies that Ben had. It would take her a long time before she wanted to lounge on that hull.

"I'm glad he's happy here. Are you? Are you staying?" Amanda fidgeted with the bag of dog treats and tried to pretend the answer didn't mean everything to her.

"The others were just asking me that. I'm staying. And I'm going to keep the boat for now. Having you take Qbert with you during the day has been so helpful. I don't know if you realize it, but you haven't charged me in weeks." Ben motioned for her to follow him.

"It's fine. I'm just happy to be able to help you out, and it's good to have a friend." Amanda blushed.

They stepped back outside and joined the others.

"If you all will excuse us for a minute, I want to show Amanda her surprise before it gets too dark." Ben disembarked and held his hand out for her.

She accepted the help. "What surprise?"

Ben patted Albert's shoulder as they passed him in his chair and led her down the dock until she could see the marina gate. He motioned to the parking lot. "See anything familiar?"

Amanda scanned the lot, stopping when she got to the boat parking section, and saw a big pink RV with burnt floppy ears and a newly crushed nose. "You had it towed here?"

"I had it repaired and driven here. They were able to fix the engine and brakes, but they couldn't repair the cosmetic damage to the nose without removing the whole front end of the Pink Pup, and it wouldn't look like a big dog anymore. So, I told them to leave it. It's operational and road safe. Ready for you to start work again."

"Ben, I can't afford this."

"Because you keep forgetting to ask people to pay you. So, call it back pay or a welcome gift. You've been a great friend, and I want to make sure you have what you need to stay in Ocean Wood." Ben held out the keychain with the key to her grooming RV.

Amanda was stunned. She had been so worried about doing everything she could to make sure Ben would want to stay in Ocean Wood, she had no idea he felt the same way about her.

With a squeak, Amanda jumped up and wrapped her arms around Ben's neck. He held her tight. When they finally let go, Amanda wanted to race out to the parking lot and check over the van for herself. But there would be plenty of time to do that later.

Ben kept his arm around Amanda's shoulders as they headed back. When they arrived, he stood next to Albert and cleared his throat. "I want to thank everyone for joining me tonight to celebrate my new home. You've all been so welcoming since I arrived in Ocean Wood."

Dottie and Albert applauded.

Frank held his hands out towards them. "You and

Amanda have been a colorful addition to our group. I don't know what we'd do without you both now."

Amanda blushed and reached out to squeeze Frank's hand.

Ben smiled so wide his black-framed glasses wiggled on his cheeks. Then he dropped his arm and dug into his pocket again. "Amanda, I almost forgot... I still have Alexandra's house key. Thank you for letting me stay with you while the boat was being repaired."

Amanda accepted the keychain. The thin strip of metal with the alphabet on it caught her eye. "Wait a minute."

"What's wrong?"

Amanda scanned the letters. There were two alphabets, and the second one had scrambled letters. She held the keychain up to the fading light for a closer look. "Ben, I think this is the key for the cipher in my sister's casebook."

Ben looked over her shoulder. "It just looks like a short bookmark." He grabbed her arm. "Don't rush off now."

Amanda knew Ben was joking, but she had to admit that had been her first instinct.

The sun had disappeared on the horizon, and the twinkle lights Ben had wound around the deck cast a warm glow over her friends. A gentle breeze buffeted them, and the marina's boat masts sounded like wind chimes as they climbed back onto Ben's boat. He brought out another platter of food and passed out small plates.

"You make all this in that little galley kitchen? Are you hiding elves in there that do all your cleaning?" Dot giggled and patted Albert, who squeezed her fingers and smiled.

Ben laughed. "No, I picked this up at the Lighthouse Pub after I stopped at the station to see if there was anything more on the case."

"Have they arrested the skipper?" Amanda held her breath as she waited for Ben's response. Detective Kim and another officer had taken a thorough statement from her but hadn't told her anything they had learned.

"Captain Cook has been arrested, and they have evidence against him for both murders. They found a white ceramic knife with traces of both his and Robin's blood on it in the kitchen of the yacht."

Amanda sagged with relief.

Dot scrunched up her face. "Why didn't he get rid of the shirt?"

"He couldn't. We found Robin's body so fast that he barely had time to change and hide the shirt and glove. After that, the police were monitoring the marina and checking everything and everyone going in and out."

"What did they find out about the watches?"

"You were right. Those watches weren't fake. They start in value at $50,000 each and go up from there. I had millions of dollars in watches strapped to the bottom of my boat."

Frank shook his head. "Well, that would be worth killing for. Rocky fessed up to me that his daughter didn't give him the watch. He bought both of them off Tobias and gifted one of them to Alan Erling to get his help in procuring the donation for the park."

Ben shrugged. "Well, that backfired. The police have confiscated both of their watches."

Dot snorted. "Since I was a teenager, Rocky Shore has been a pain in my—"

Albert cleared his throat.

"I was going to say 'Astern.'" Dot pursed her lips at Albert. "By the way, we didn't find any evidence of spearfishing gear thefts, which isn't surprising now we know it was Robin and the captain doing all the break-ins as they searched for the watches."

"Tell them the other thing we learned," Albert encouraged her.

Dot jumped up again. "Oh yeah, you won't believe this. We found out Silver from the Electric Sandwich will be playing at the Butterfly Music and Art Festival. Tickets go on sale this week. You're both coming, right?" Dot nodded to Ben and Amanda.

Amanda hesitated. She didn't know what the others would think of this. "Actually, when I was talking to Silver, he promised me two tickets and a backstage tour at his next show. I guess that would be the festival."

Dot stared. "I can't believe you have backstage passes. I'd rip my blouse off for those."

Amanda choked out a gasping laugh. "You're kidding?"

Albert shook his head and chuckled. "Wouldn't be the first time."

Amanda laughed, and Frank started a story about the time he camped in a rainstorm to get the front row at a Silver concert.

Grok wandered down from the hull of the boat and joined them, lying across the back of the sun bed. As Amanda threaded fingers through his hair and the cat purred, she realized how lucky she was to have found this group and a new home in Ocean Wood.

Now, if only she could find her sister.

THE END

Join the newsletter for bonus chapters and hear about new releases and free books: https://www.serengoode.com/cozybooks-nlt

Thank you!

Your comments and feedback are so important to me and they help other readers select a book they will enjoy. **If you liked this book, please spread the word! Leave a review** on the platform where you bought it or on **Goodreads** or **Bookbub**. And thank you for telling your friends and posting on social!

We would love to have you join our community of cozy mystery readers. Sign-up to engage, share ideas, receive news, hear about future books, get free stories and lots of fun stuff through (mostly) monthly emails...and no spam. https://www.serengoode.com/cozybooks-nlt.

And if you love talking about the books you read, then consider joining the **Cozy Mystery Books Review (ARC) Team**. You can sign-up at https://www.seren goode.com/contact

I sincerely appreciate your support and would love to hear from you at SerenGoodWrites on:

Contact https://www.serengoode.com/contact
Goodreads http://bit.ly/Goodreads_SerenGoode
Bookbub http://bit.ly/BookBub_SerenGoode
Instagram instagram.com/serengoodewrites
TikTok tiktok.com/@serengoodewrites
Facebook facebook.com/SerenGoode
Pinterest pinterest.com/SerenGoodeWrites

Other books by Seren Goode
The Elements Series (Young Adult)
The Keystone
The Activator
Amanda Warren Cozy Animal Mystery Series (Mystery)
Monterey Bay Mystery
Monterey Bay Murder

Acknowledgments

It takes a lot of support to be an author and I want to thank all my family and friends that have helped me along the way. I especially want to thank Randy for always having my back. Amy C. for coaching and cohosting. My Tropetastic friends. Hannah J. for editing and the tough talks. Bob Walker for his insights on marinas, boats, and sailing. And my personal cheerleader who got me into this whole cozy business and is the most fabulous beta reader and friend, Lori Henderson.

Thank you!

Any mistakes in this story are my own.

About the Author

Seren Goode was born in the Midwest with itchy feet and dreams of far-off places. She loves travel and walking on the beach while the fog rolls in. No matter where she is in the world her favorite thing is curling up with a cozy mystery book and a hot cup of tea.

A Jane-of-all-trades, Seren has studied English, design, marketing, metalsmithing, pottery, juggling, and archeology. She started writing fiction while in middle school and thoroughly blames her family for encouraging this habit. A big fan of making her characters do their own work, Seren loves to sit back and watch them unravel a mystery or dig for the truth. When she isn't on the road, she is at home on the Central Coast of California, plotting her next book and her next trip with her songwriter husband and puppies, Clairey and Izzy.

You can follow her at serengoode.com or on:
facebook.com/SerenGoode
instagram.com/serengoodewrites
pinterest.com/SerenGoodeWrites
tiktok.com/@serengoodewrites

Monterey Bay Murder

Written and published by Seren Goode

Cover by Mariah Sinclair & Associates

Formatting by Goode Star

Copyright © 2024 by W.S. Goodman, Seren Goode, Goode Star Publishing, All rights reserved.

Ebook ISBN: 978-1-7365387-8-4

Print ISBN: 978-1-7365387-9-1

No part of this book may be reproduced in any form or by any electronic or mechanical means, including information storage and retrieval systems, without written permission from the author, except for the use of brief quotations in a book review.

This is a work of fiction. Any resemblance to actual events, places, or persons, living or dead, is entirely coincidental.

SerenGoode.com

www.ingramcontent.com/pod-product-compliance
Lightning Source LLC
Chambersburg PA
CBHW051139190726
48290CB00006B/1918